# "Who's that man?"

Phil peered past her. "Oh, that's Blake Fowler." He gave her a knowing smile and raised an eyebrow. "Why? Are you interested in him? If so, you'll have to stand in line. He has quite a reputation as a man-about-town."

"Interested in him?" Shelley spluttered. "He's the most boorish man I've ever run across!"

Rosemary Hammond grew up in California, but has since lived in several other states. Rosemary and her husband have traveled extensively throughout the United States, Mexico, the Caribbean and Canada, both with and without their two sons. She started writing romances because she enjoyed them, but also because the mechanics of fiction fascinated her and she thought they might be something she could do. She also enjoys gardening, music and needlework, but her greatest pleasure has always been reading.

## Books by Rosemary Hammond

**HARLEQUIN ROMANCE**

# THE POWER OF LOVE
## Rosemary Hammond

## *Harlequin Books*

TORONTO • NEW YORK • LONDON
AMSTERDAM • PARIS • SYDNEY • HAMBURG
STOCKHOLM • ATHENS • TOKYO • MILAN
MADRID • WARSAW • BUDAPEST • AUCKLAND

ISBN 0-373-17218-4

THE POWER OF LOVE

# CHAPTER ONE

SHELLEY gazed raptly up at the man on the podium, her ears tuned into every word that dropped from his lips. He was warming to his subject now, hitting his stride, turning on the old Carruthers charm. In a moment he would reach the point he'd been building up to and half blast his audience out of their seats.

She was convinced there was no question now that he'd be elected in November. The polls had shown him steadily creeping up on his opponent, the incumbent, since early summer, catching up by August, and now, in September, finally passing him by.

The next governor! And as his secretary first, then later on as a member of his public relations team, she'd had a large part in his successful campaign. He had the audience eating out of his hand now, with him every step of the way as he reached the climax of his talk, his five-point plan for the future of the state.

Just then, at the crucial moment, the man sitting next to her stifled a deep, audible yawn. He'd been restive throughout the entire speech, shuffling his feet, shifting around in his chair, twiddling his thumbs, even at one point humming a little under his breath, and by now Shelley had had enough. She swivelled her head around to give him her nastiest look. Unfortunately the auditorium was so dark he couldn't see it, but it did make her feel better.

Then it was over. There was a loud burst of applause, a few cheers, and Jim Carruthers, bowing and smiling, his silvery grey hair gleaming under the bright lights, took his seat. As the clapping died down, once again the man next to her was heard from.

'Thank God,' she heard him mutter feelingly.

The house lights came up just then, and she turned to him. 'I beg your pardon?' she said in a stiff challenging tone.

'I said, ''Thank God,'' ' he repeated in a louder voice. 'That it's finally over, I mean.'

She looked down her nose at him, hoping to intimidate him, and was about to deliver a scathing rebuttal, but stopped just in time. There was no point in antagonising a prospective voter, and she might learn something that would help in the campaign.

'I take it you don't agree with Jim Carruthers' platform,' she said in a carefully neutral tone.

'Platform!' he exclaimed. 'Do you call that load of twaddle a platform? A six-year-old has more insight into the workings of government than Carruthers ever did or ever will. He hasn't had an original thought in his entire life. The man's a walking puppet, and it's common knowledge who pulls the strings.'

Shelley was having real difficulty now in holding her temper, especially since his last comment came uncomfortably close to a hidden concern of her own. 'Then why do you bother to come and listen to him speak?' she asked in a deceptively sweet tone.

He rose to his feet and looked down at her. 'It's part of my job—one of the least pleasant aspects of it, I might add.' He narrowed his eyes at her. 'Say, don't I know you?'

She stood up beside him and gazed up into a pair of the most piercing blue eyes she'd ever seen. 'I doubt it,' she said tartly. Picking up her handbag, she turned her back on him and moved away down the aisle.

Half an hour later she was in the ballroom next to the auditorium standing at the end of the reception line and watching the steady stream of well-wishers inching forward to greet the silver-haired candidate. Next to her was Phil Dorsey, her immediate boss, a shaggy-looking young man who knew everything there was to know about winning elections, Jim Carruthers' right-hand man.

'Great crowd,' she said to him. 'And a warm reception too, didn't you think?'

'Not bad,' he said guardedly. 'But it's still early days, two months before the election. Anything can happen.' He gave her a rather wistful look. 'I wish we could get the *News-Tribune* to come out in support of Jim.'

'Well, at least they haven't endorsed the other side,' she said in an optimistic tone. 'And we do seem to have the Talbot newspaper sewn up tight.'

'Yes, but I wonder if Jim might not find that getting Talbot's support carries a pretty high price.' Phil laughed drily and nodded at the tall, willowy blonde woman standing next to Jim Carruthers in the reception line. 'It looks as though the lovely

Vanessa has already taken her place as lady of the manor.'

Shelley twisted her head around and gave him a sharp look. 'That's only a courtesy. It doesn't mean anything.'

Phil raised his sandy eyebrows. 'Oh, no?' He grinned. 'Only that with Daddy's newspaper behind him, not to mention the big bucks he's throwing into the campaign, Jim's put himself under pretty heavy obligation to the Talbot clan.'

Shelley lifted her shoulders in an offhand shrug. 'Well, I guess you can't blame him for that.'

'Who's blaming him? Vanessa may not be my cup of tea, but she'll make a damned good governor's wife.'

'I think you're jumping to conclusions, Phil,' she replied in a tight voice.

She turned away from him and gazed blankly at the crowd. Phil didn't say anything for a few moments, but she could feel his eyes upon her. Finally he bent down to put his mouth close to her ear.

'You know, Shelley,' he said in a low voice, 'you could have had a shot at him if you'd tried.' She jerked her head around again and stared at him. 'I mean,' he went on with a shrug, 'a beautiful girl like you. You have it all over Vanessa in looks and brains, in every department as far as I'm concerned. Why you hide behind those dumb glasses, blah hairstyle and frumpy suits beats me.'

Shelley felt herself reddening, but didn't say anything. That was a subject she didn't intend to discuss with anyone, not even Phil, who had been her friend and mentor since the beginning of Jim's campaign almost a year ago, when he'd announced his candidacy. She couldn't tell him the real reason for the glasses she didn't really need, the severe hairstyle, the drab suits.

She'd been in love with Jim Carruthers since the first day she'd gone to work for him as his secretary four years ago. He'd been the district attorney then, and working for him had lifted her out of the dull existence she'd fallen into since the failure of her youthful marriage a year earlier. He'd been the first man who had even remotely interested her since that shattering experience, and when she had finally admitted it to herself she had fallen hard.

Until he'd decided to run for governor, in fact, she'd been almost certain he felt the same way about her. Their relationship had steadily progressed from boss-secretary to friendly dinners together to a few tentative kisses. But all that had changed when Jim had thrown his hat in the governor's ring. He'd never spelled it out to her, but somehow she'd known instinctively that to get the support of the powerful Talbot newspapers he would be expected to play along with Vanessa Talbot, and that meant Shelley would have to take a back seat and don a less threatening image.

The severe chignon at the back of her neck neutralised her vibrant auburn hair, the horn-rimmed glasses dulled her bright green eyes, and the tailored suits cloaked a figure that bordered on the voluptuous. It was worth it, she kept telling herself, to get Jim elected. Then everything would change. In the meantime, however, Vanessa Talbot was becoming more and more possessive, and, although Shelley wouldn't admit it to Phil for the world, it gave her a decided pang to see the blonde standing beside Jim, hanging on to him, smiling graciously, just as though she belonged there.

Resolving to banish such troublesome thoughts, she fixed her gaze firmly on the people still in line waiting to meet Jim. Among them she recognised the man who had sat next to her during the speech. Even at a distance those blue eyes of his gleamed, and as he approached she noticed how tall he was, much taller than she remembered. He was well dressed in a dark suit, white shirt and tie, and had a thick head of coal-black hair.

She nudged Phil. 'Who's that man?' she muttered *sotto voce*. 'The tall dark-haired one just behind Senator Jared and his wife.'

Phil peered past her. 'Oh, that's Blake Fowler. He owns the *News-Tribune.*' He gave her a knowing smile and raised an eyebrow. 'Why? Are you interested in him? If so, you'll have to stand in line. He has quite a reputation as a man about town.'

'Interested in him?' she hissed. 'He's the most boorish man I've ever run across!'

'Oh? In what way?'

'I was sitting next to him during Jim's speech, and his comments about it were not flattering, to put it mildly.'

Phil laughed. 'No, he's not one of Jim's greatest fans. Too bad. We could use his paper's support.'

'Hasn't the *News-Tribune* stayed pretty much on the fence? I mean, they haven't really endorsed either candidate yet, have they?'

'No, but if Fowler decided to support Jim the election would be sewn up tight.' He gave her a considered look. 'No chance you might try to influence him in that direction, is there?'

'Are you kidding? The man's a . . .'

Phil gripped her arm tightly, cutting her off. 'Not so loud,' he whispered. 'Here he comes.'

The tall dark man had just shaken hands with Jim Carruthers, said a few words to Vanessa Talbot, and was now ambling down the receiving line, heading straight for them, an inscrutable half-smile playing about his lips and a gleam of recognition in the startling blue eyes as they fell on Shelley.

'Hello, Dorsey,' he said, turning to Phil. 'Quite an enthusiastic crowd you have here tonight.'

'Yes, isn't it?' Phil replied, beaming. 'What brings you here, Blake?'

'Oh, just curiosity.'

'I see. I was hoping your august presence might mean your paper has decided to jump off the fence and land on our side.'

The tall man smiled noncommittally and his eyes flicked back at Shelley. 'Hello again,' he said smoothly.

Before she could say anything, Phil had grabbed her by the arm and was squeezing it tight. 'This is Shelley Dalton, my assistant.' Still hanging on to her arm, he gave her a warning smile. 'Shelley, I'd like you to meet Blake Fowler.'

'How do you do, Mr Fowler?' Shelley murmured.

'Miss Dalton,' the man returned with a nod.

Phil finally released her arm. 'Are you staying for the festivities, Blake?' he asked. 'If so,' he went on in a rush, 'why don't you join our party?'

'Yes, I had intended to stay, but I'm meeting friends.' He glanced around at the crowd, which was now drifting towards the tables placed around the dance-floor. 'In fact, I see them now.' He turned back to Phil. 'Nice to have seen you, Phil. Miss Dalton.'

With that he turned and strode away from them, his hands in his trouser pockets, heading for one of the larger tables in front of the bandstand, where a group of people were already seated. Shelley watched as he stopped behind the chair of a dark-haired woman and put his hands on her shoulders. The woman turned her head and smiled up at him, covering his hands with her own, then he sat down beside her and bent his head towards hers.

Shelley turned and frowned at Phil. 'Did you have to grab my arm quite so hard?' she demanded. 'What did you think I was going to do, for heaven's sake?'

'With you, my dear Shelley, I'm never quite sure. You're like a lioness guarding her cubs when it comes to Jim Carruthers. I wasn't going to take any chances that you might decide to give Blake a piece of that sharp mind of yours for daring to criticise your hero's speech.'

'Oh, come on,' protested Shelley, stung by the comparison. 'I'm not that bad. Just because I believe in Jim, what he stands for, it doesn't mean I'm blind to the fact that he's not everybody's cup of tea. And in any case, you surely ought to know I have sense enough not to antagonise a man like Blake Fowler.'

'Well, all right, I apologise.' He put his chin in his hand, rubbing it thoughtfully. 'I wonder what Fowler was really doing here tonight? Could be he really is thinking about supporting Jim.'

'After the remarks he made about his speech?' Shelley said. 'I think you're dreaming, Phil. And

I notice he neatly side-stepped your question about his intentions.' She shook her head slowly. 'I don't think it's going to happen.'

'Well, in politics, one never knows.' He gave her a disarming grin. 'Come on, I see the others are already at the table. We'd better join them, or they'll think we've decided to elope.'

'Ha!' Shelley snorted. 'Fat chance of that!'

Phil gave her a hurt look. 'Well, thanks a lot! I thought you found me irresistible.'

'Oh, I do,' she replied, smiling up at him. 'I don't know how I could do without you. You've taught me all I know about politics.'

'Thanks again.' He took her arm, lightly this time, and they headed towards Jim's table.

Two hours later Shelley was more than ready to go home. She'd been up since dawn helping Phil prepare for tonight's event. It was Jim's major speech, the most important one in the campaign so far, and it was critical that everything go off smoothly.

Now her feet hurt, her head was throbbing, every bone in her body ached, and all she wanted to do was go home, soak in a hot tub and get to bed. She'd had her one dance with Jim, which was all she'd get, she knew, with the possessive Vanessa watching every move he made, and that would have to satisfy her.

Tomorrow was another busy day, and if she didn't get some sleep she didn't see how she could face it. She looked around the table. Phil was involved in a deep discussion with Vanessa's father, Jim and Vanessa were dancing, and the two other couples present, friends of the Talbots, looked as tired as she felt. Surely no one would miss her if she slipped away.

She was just about to lean over and tap Phil on the shoulder to tell him she was leaving when she heard a voice behind her speaking her name. 'Miss Dalton—Shelley.'

She twisted around in her chair and looked up to see Blake Fowler standing there looking down at her. 'Oh, it's you,' she said. She forced out a smile. 'Were you speaking to me?'

'Yes,' he replied. 'I asked you if you'd like to dance.'

'Oh, I'm sorry, Mr Fowler, I was just leaving.'

'Surely you can spare the time for one dance,' he persisted.

She felt Phil's elbow nudging her in the ribs. 'Go on, Shelley,' he prompted with a meaningful smile. 'You don't have to leave just yet. The night's still young.'

'Maybe for you,' she retorted tartly, giving him a dirty look. 'But I'm dead beat.'

'Well, one more dance won't hurt you, will it?' he said through his teeth, his voice pitched so low that only she could hear it.

She knew what he was trying to do, of course— fob her off on to Blake Fowler in the hope of interesting the man in the campaign—but she felt that was pushing duty far beyond its natural limits. She didn't like the man, didn't believe there was a chance in hell of his supporting Jim in any circumstances, and she wanted to go home.

Just then Jim and Vanessa danced by and stopped at the table. 'Blake, nice to see you're still here,' Jim said smoothly. 'Anything we can do for you?'

'Well, you can talk your friend here into dancing with me. She doesn't seem to be interested.'

Jim gazed benevolently down at Shelley. 'She's only kidding, aren't you, Shelley?' He beamed at Blake. 'Wonderful sense of humour, our Shelley.'

Shelley knew when she was beaten. There was very little she wouldn't do for Jim Carruthers, and he knew it. Sighing inwardly, she rose slowly to her feet and turned around to face Blake Fowler with a smile she didn't feel.

'That's right,' she said evenly. 'I was only kidding. I'd be happy to dance with you, Mr Fowler.'

'Blake, please,' he murmured. He took her by the hand, then put his other arm around her and swept her out on to the dance-floor.

He turned out to be a marvellous dancer for such a big man. His hold around her waist was firm, his step sure and smooth. While they danced he made no effort at conversation, but hummed lightly under his breath along with orchestra, which was playing an old show tune, and in time Shelley found she was quite enjoying herself.

'So,' he said finally, 'you're a member of Jim Carruthers' team.'

'Yes,' she replied. 'Although in a minor capacity. Phil Dorsey is the man in charge.'

'You might have told me,' he said in a mildly chiding tone. 'Back there after the speech when I was so free with my opinions.'

'I might have,' she said evenly. 'But would it have made a difference to your opinions?'

He shrugged and gave her a look full of meaning. 'Who knows?' Then he laughed. 'Probably not. I must say I'm rather surprised, though.'

'At what?'

'Well, I know that politics makes strange bed-fellows, but you seem like a sensible girl, all decked out in your correct little black suit, those businesslike glasses.' He frowned. 'Do you really need them to dance?'

'Why, no, not really.'

'Then why don't you take them off? You shouldn't hide those marvellous green eyes of yours behind them.'

Before she could think of a reply the music stopped suddenly. When he made no move to let go her hand or remove his arm from around her waist, Shelley gave him an enquiring look. To her surprise, he was gazing down at her intently, his features set in a slightly puzzled frown.

'What is it?' she asked.

'What's what?' was the reply.

She laughed. 'From the way you're staring at me I thought I must have a smudge on my face or something.'

He returned the smile, revealing very even, very white teeth, and shook his head. 'No,' he said with a slow shake of his head, 'nothing like that. I'm just wondering why such a lovely-looking woman takes such pains to hide her looks.'

Shelley flushed deeply and drew back a step from him. 'I don't know what you're talking about,' she murmured.

'Oh, come on, now.' He put a hand under her chin and tilted her face up to his, the blue, blue eyes scanning her carefully. 'That glorious hair, for example,' he said in a low intimate tone. 'It's just the colour the maples turn in the autumn—a deep russet, I'd call it.' His hand moved upwards to brush over the loose bun at the back of her neck, and he frowned. 'Why tuck it away like that? It should be hanging loose to your shoulders. And with your skin,' he added, 'the shoulders definitely should be bare.'

The low, soothing tone of his voice had an almost hypnotic effect on her. It had been a long time since a man had looked at her like that, with such frank appreciation, or said such things to her. Just at that moment the band started playing again. Another couple on the floor jostled against them, and she gave herself a little shake, jolted back into the real world.

'Well, be that as it may,' she said crisply. 'Now, I did enjoy the dance, but...'

Before she could finish the sentence, he had put his arm back around her and started to dance off with her again. This time he held her more tightly, pressing his cheek up against hers, his warm breath in her ear.

By now she was beginning to feel slightly irritated at the whole situation. Being pleasant to Blake Fowler for Jim's sake was one thing, but putting up with such a blatant come-on quite another. She was exhausted, her feet still hurt, and the last thing she felt like doing was dancing away what was left of the night in the arms of this man, who obviously had only one thing on his mind.

As they danced by Jim's table, she saw to her horror that not a soul was sitting there. They'd all

gone home and left her here to fend for herself!
Her irritation escalated into a simmering anger, and
she simply stopped short and stood there, so that
Blake almost bumped right into her.

He gave her a quizzical look. 'What's up?'

'I'm very tired, Blake,' she said in a reasonable
tone. She even managed a wan smile. 'It's been a
long day, and I really think it's time I went home.'

To her surprise, he only nodded. 'Sure,' he said,
releasing her. 'I understand.'

She'd been expecting a battle, and was so relieved at his easy acceptance of her wishes that her
anger evaporated on the spot. 'Well, it was nice to
meet you, Blake. Perhaps we'll see each other
around...'

But he wasn't paying any attention to her. 'Is this
yours?' he asked, removing the jacket of her black
suit from the back of the chair where she'd left it.

'Why, yes, it is,' she replied, reaching for it.

He held it up for her, and she turned round to
slip her arms into the sleeves. After settling it on
her shoulders, however, he kept his hands firmly
in place and bent his head down next to hers.

'Let's go,' he said. 'I'll see you home.'

Startled, she whirled around to face him. 'No!'
she exclaimed. Then, in a calmer voice, she went
on, 'No, but thanks anyway. I can find my own
way home. Besides, what about your party?'

He waved a hand dismissively in the air. 'Oh,
they're just business associates.'

Shelley recalled the dark-haired woman at his
table, the way his hands had rested on her
shoulders, how she'd smiled at him. If that was how

he treated his business associates, it must be a very friendly group indeed!

'There's really no need,' she tried again.

'Nonsense,' he said, taking her firmly by the arm and steering her towards the door. 'You shouldn't be out on the city streets alone at this time of night—it's dangerous.'

Shelley gritted her teeth. Not half so dangerous as you, Mr Blake Fowler, she muttered silently as she allowed herself to be propelled along at his side.

All during the taxi ride to her apartment, Blake kept up a running commentary on the many changes that had occurred in the Seattle skyline over the past few years, while Shelley huddled in her corner making polite replies and trying to think up ways to steer the subject towards Jim's bid for election. So long as she was stuck with him, she might as well try to get some good out of it.

Finally there was a lull in the conversation and she saw her chance. 'Tell me,' she said, turning to him, 'what have you really got against Jim?'

He shrugged. 'Oh, nothing tangible. I guess I just don't like—or trust—politicians. You'll notice my paper isn't supporting his opponent either.'

'Well, whether you like them or not, they're part of our system, and surely a powerful influence on public opinion like your newspaper has an obligation to take a stand in such an important election, even if it means supporting the lesser of two evils.'

He stared at her for a long moment, eyes widened, and even in the dimness the blue of them glowed. 'You really care, don't you?' he said at last.

'Well, yes, I do. And I think Jim will make a fine governor.'

'Is that opinion based on his qualities of leadership?' he asked. 'Or do I detect a more personal note in your enthusiasm?'

'I'm not sure exactly what you're driving at,' she replied heatedly, 'but I want to assure you I'm working for Jim because I believe in him. If I like and respect him as a person, that's only part of the package.'

'All right,' he conceded equably. 'If you say so. It's a good thing, too.'

'Why is that?' Shelley asked stiffly.

'Only that it looks to me as though on a personal level Vanessa Talbot has him sewed up pretty tight. And with Daddy's newspaper and financial support in the background, Carruthers needs to play her game, at least until after the election. I know Vanessa rather well, and she's a tigress when it comes to keeping potential rivals away from her property.'

'That's not fair!' she retorted heatedly. 'And Jim's not Vanessa's property.'

'Oh, no?' Blake let the question hang in the air for a few moments, then moved an inch or two closer to her. 'But let's not talk about Jim Carruthers any more. I never like to mix business with pleasure.'

They weren't quite touching, but she was intensely aware of his proximity all the same, and she sat there stiffly, clutching her handbag in her lap, wondering how in the world she was going to beat him off without offending him. They ought to give courses on it in school, she thought bitterly.

Luckily, before he could make his move, the taxi pulled up to the kerb in front of her building. They both got out, and she braced herself for a battle on her doorstep. But then, to her surprise, she heard Blake tell the driver to wait for him.

They walked together to the entrance and he waited while she unlocked the door, but clearly had no intention of trying to force his way inside.

She turned back to him. 'Well, goodnight, Blake,' she said. 'And thanks for seeing me home.'

'My pleasure.' He braced a hand against the door-frame and leaned down to brush his lips lightly over her forehead, then straightened up. 'I'd like to see you again, Shelley,' he said.

'Oh, I'm sorry, Blake,' she replied quickly, 'but these last several weeks before the election are going to be so hectic for me, I'm afraid I won't have any spare time to speak of.'

'All right,' he said. 'I won't push it.' He stepped back from her. 'Good luck with the campaign.' He grinned. 'And may the best man win.'

With a little salute, he turned around and strode jauntily away from her, his hands in his trousers pockets, whistling lightly. Shelley watched while he got back into the waiting taxi, and after it drove off she turned and went slowly inside her apartment.

The whole episode puzzled her. Why had he come on so strong, with all that seductive nonsense about her hair and eyes and skin, then backed off so easily when she'd turned him down? A man like Blake Fowler certainly couldn't be used to rejection, but it didn't seem to bother him in the slightest. He'd just shrugged it off, taken her at her word, and walked off.

She went into the bathroom, switched on the light and gazed into the mirror. She took off her glasses, then slowly unpinned her hair, running her fingers through it until it fell loosely to her shoulders in its natural wave.

She stared dreamily at her reflection, recalling vividly what he'd said—that with her skin her shoulders should be bare. Then abruptly she came to her senses, made a face at herself and switched off the light. What a stupid thing to get all dewy-eyed about! Not only was Jim Carruthers her ideal of masculine perfection, she didn't even like the man. He was arrogant, overbearing and far too sure of himself.

Nor did she at all like the way he'd implied that Jim's relationship with Vanessa Talbot was a crass bid for her father's money and influence. Yet a little seed of doubt had been planted. How else to explain the way Jim had danced attendance on the lovely blonde?

Just then the telephone shrilled, breaking into the silence. She ran into the living-room to answer it, hoping it would be Jim. But instead Phil's voice came through loud and clear.

'Well?' he demanded.

'Well what?'

'What happened between you and Fowler?'

'Nothing,' she replied shortly. 'And thanks a lot for leaving me in the lurch like that.'

'How else would he ask to see you home? He did take you home, didn't he?'

'Yes,' she said slowly. Something was wrong here. She thought carefully for a moment, then said, 'Phil, what's going on? Do you have some diabolical scheme up your sleeve you're not telling me about?'

'Who, me?'

She could just see the deceptively boyish grin on his face, and was not in the least amused, knowing quite well that a piranha lurked underneath it. 'Then why all the interest in shoving me off on Blake Fowler like that?'

'Well, he was obviously interested in you, and we could use his support.'

'Phil,' she said, enunciating clearly as if to a child, 'you're not suggesting...'

'Hey, hold on! I'm not suggesting anything.'

'Because if you are, you can forget it. Besides, Jim would never condone my—my—*prostituting* myself to help get him elected.'

There was dead silence on the line for several long seconds, then Blake spoke again in a low, soft voice. 'Are you really so sure of that, Shelley?'

'I'm going to forget you said that, Phil,' she stated firmly, really angry by now. 'I'll see you at the meeting tomorrow morning. Goodbye.'

She replaced the receiver in its cradle, very gently, for fear she'd slam it down in his ear if she let herself go. Her hand was shaking by now, her teeth clenched together, and if Phil had been there at that moment she would have thrown the telephone at him.

'How dare he?' she said aloud as she stalked off to her bedroom. 'I'll kill him if he ever even hints at such a thing again!'

But in the small hours of the morning, as she lay still wakeful in her bed, that last question came back to haunt her. *Was* she so sure Jim would object to her having an affair with Blake Fowler if it would help get him elected?

# CHAPTER TWO

THE next morning at the weekly policy meeting in Jim's office, the question still nagged at Shelley's mind. But now, in the light of a sunny day, she knew the answer. Jim Carruthers was an honourable man. He would never ask her to do anything against her conscience just for the sake of an election.

As for Vanessa Talbot, why shouldn't he be nice to her? Both she and her father were doing a great deal to help him. It was only natural that he'd feel obliged to squire her around at various political functions. That didn't mean he was going to marry her, or anything like that. She might be decorative and a public asset to Jim in some ways, but when it came down to the finer details of planning the campaign it was Shelley he relied on and trusted.

After an hour's discussion of Jim's speaking engagements and public appearances for the next week, the conversation turned to the latest polls, which still showed the two candidates virtually tied, with Jim marginally ahead of his opponent.

'What we really need is to widen that gap,' Phil said. 'And an endorsement from Blake Fowler's newspaper would turn the tide overnight, send us so far ahead, the other side would never catch up.'

Shelley, who had been taking notes of the meeting, was suddenly aware that there was a dead silence in the room. She looked up from her notebook to see both men staring at her. She sat up a little straighter and glanced warily from one to the other.

Phil had that closed-in, blank-eyed expression on his face that meant he was hatching a brand-new scheme, and Jim was leaning back in his chair, his hands clasped under his chin, his eyes half closed. The thoughtful look on his handsome features told her the wheels were turning in his head too.

'Well, don't look at me!' she said at last. She glared at Phil. 'You told me to be nice to him last night, and I was. I don't know what more you want.'

She glanced at Jim. He was bending towards her, one hand outstretched, placing it lightly on her arm. At his touch, the old helpless love for him rose up to melt her heart and addle her wits.

'Now, Shelley,' he said in his rich soothing baritone, 'we don't want you to do one thing that might be distasteful to you in any way. You must believe me. Isn't that right, Phil?'

'Oh, you bet,' Phil agreed quickly. 'Naturally not. But this is politics, baby,' he went on, turning to Shelley. 'We have to use whatever weapons we've got.' He shrugged. 'Blake Fowler was obviously quite taken with you. To you, that might be distasteful, but to me it's an asset we could use to help get Jim elected.'

'But he's already ahead!' she protested. 'Why do we need the *News-Tribune*'s support?'

'We could lose that edge in the twinkling of an eye,' Phil said, snapping his fingers to emphasise his point.

Shelley sat there silently for a moment or two, staring out of the window at the traffic going by on the busy city street, mulling over the implications of what Phil was saying. The same pattern was repeated at every meeting. It was always Phil who made the most objectionable proposals. He'd been the one who had encouraged Jim to take advantage of Vanessa's interest in him, and now he was trying to convince her to play the same game with Blake Fowler.

'You do want to see Jim elected, don't you?' Phil asked.

She turned her head slowly to meet his gaze. 'Of course I do,' she replied. 'It's why I'm here, isn't it?'

Phil spread his hands. 'Well then here's something really important you can do. Something *only* you can do.'

She frowned. 'It just seems so underhanded.' Then she heaved a deep sigh. 'All right, just what is it you want me to do?'

'That's my girl,' Phil said, beaming. He leaned forward eagerly. 'We've invited Fowler to the reception tonight at the Talbot penthouse. All you have to do is be pleasant to him.'

'How do you know he'll even come?'

'Oh, he'll come. How did you leave things last night?'

'Well, he asked to see me again.'

'And what did you say?'

'I told him the truth,' she said with a defensive lift to her chin. 'That I'd be too busy between now and the election.'

Phil rolled his eyes and groaned. 'Big mistake, Shelley.'

'Well, how was I to know you planned on throwing me at him like this? I mean, Phil, the man's a predator, only interested in one thing—surely you know that? You seem to know everything else. Just how far do you expect me to go with this little charade?'

She was growing really angry by now, at Phil mostly, but at Jim too, who was simply sitting silently by letting Phil do all his dirty work for him. She'd thought he really cared for her. How could he let Phil push her into encouraging a man like Blake Fowler?

'Jim?' she appealed to him. 'What do you think?'

Jim shrugged and looked down at his hands. 'Phil's the expert here, Shelley,' he muttered at last. 'It's what we pay him for.'

'Shelley, Shelley,' Phil broke in, his voice low and soothing. 'We're not asking you to go to bed with the guy, for God's sake.'

Her green eyes flashed at him. 'Just what else do you think he wants?' she snapped.

'You can always say no, if it comes to that,' Phil replied.

She folded her arms across her chest and glared at him. 'Yes, so long as it's after the election, I suppose.'

No one said anything for several long moments, and her words just hung in the air between them. Shelley's mind raced. What should she do? Here was an opportunity to help the man she loved. But it meant deception, and everything in her rebelled against it.

'Listen,' Phil was saying in a reasonable tone. 'Fowler's an old hand at this game. Do you think for one minute he'd hesitate to use every means at his disposal to get something he wanted?'

'No,' she mumbled grudgingly. 'I guess not.'

'And after all, he's not exactly Frankenstein's monster. You should be flattered. There are lots of women who'd jump at the chance to be the object of Fowler's attentions. I mean, the guy's got to be one of the most powerful men in the city, with that newspaper of his.' The grin broadened. 'Not to mention that he's also a prime catch, probably *the* most eligible bachelor in town.'

'Hah!' she snorted. 'Eligible for what?'

'Then you'll do it?'

'Oh, I guess so,' she said wearily. 'I don't seem to have much choice.' She pointed a warning finger at him. 'But I call the shots, remember, and if it gets too sticky I'll back out, election or no election.'

Phil nodded emphatically. 'Right.'

Shelley glanced again from one man to the other. Phil wore a maddening smirk of satisfaction on his blunt features, while Jim still couldn't quite meet her eye. She was stuck and she knew it. There was, however, one frail hope, one last string to her bow.

'All right,' she said in a tone of resignation, 'I'll play your little game. But I still don't know what makes you two think I'll even get another chance at him. Womanisers like Blake Fowler have pretty fragile egos, and I made it quite clear last night that I didn't want to see him again. He may not rise to the bait.'

Phil threw back his head and laughed. 'Blake Fowler? A fragile ego? That's really funny, Shelley.'

He turned to Jim. 'Isn't that right, Jim? You know him better than I do.'

Jim gave Shelley a warm, encouraging smile. 'Well, all I can say is that I've never known him to give up when a beautiful woman catches his eye.'

Shelley returned his smile, warmed to the depths of her being by the compliment. If Jim thought she was beautiful, that was enough reward for her. And when the blasted election was finally over, Vanessa Talbot would disappear and she and Jim could pick up where they left off before the campaign began.

Just then Phil's voice broke into her reverie. 'Er—Shelley,' he said hesitantly, 'there is just one more thing.'

'What's that?' she snapped, immediately on guard.

'Well, I realise you like to keep a low profile, and I think it's a wise move, but maybe just for the time being you could do something to jazz up your appearance a little.'

'I don't see why,' she rejoined immediately. 'If he really is interested, as you keep telling me, it must be at least partly because of the way I look now. Why should I change it?'

Phil cocked his head on one side and gave her a conspiratorial grin. 'Well, it never hurts to put a little icing on the cake, does it?' When he saw the look on her face, he raised a hand. 'Now hold on, I'm not suggesting you doll up like a seductive siren. But you could get rid of the glasses, put on a pretty dress tonight, do something about your hair. That's all.'

Shelley rose to her feet, smoothed the skirt of her suit and gazed down her nose at him. 'We'll see,' she said. 'Now, if we're through here, I have work to do.'

At seven o'clock that evening, Shelley was in her bedroom, fresh from the shower, dressed in her robe, a towel wrapped around her wet head, and riffling through her wardrobe.

She'd been so busy all day after the morning meeting with Jim and Phil that she hadn't given the party that night another thought. Now she had to come up with something to wear to the Talbots' party, which was to be a formal affair.

As she poked through the rack of tailored suits and severe blouses, she recalled Phil's insistence that she 'put a little icing on the cake'. She frowned at the hateful term. It was almost as though he was putting her up on the auction block, for sale to the highest bidder.

The whole thing went against the grain, her deepest concept of who she was, what was right and wrong. To set out deliberately to deceive another human being, even one like Blake Fowler, who apparently had the morals of an alley cat and wouldn't hesitate to do the same to her if she gave him the chance, simply was not on. She couldn't do it.

'I can't do it,' she said aloud, and began to yank out a black velveteen suit with a long skirt that would be formal enough, even for the Talbots' exalted tastes.

Then she hesitated, her hand still on the hanger, and thought of Jim, of how much this election meant to him. It would only be for another six weeks. And she didn't have to practise a real deception, pretend she really cared about the man.

She reached further back in the wardrobe where she had stored her dressier, more feminine clothes some months back, and finally chose a simple black dress, cut in a form-fitting style that showed off her slim figure to full advantage without appearing blatantly seductive. The round neckline was cut very low, just skimming the tops of her high, firm breasts, and so wide that she couldn't wear anything with straps underneath it.

The long sleeves, buttoning at the wrist, added a more demure touch, but after putting it on and gazing critically at her reflection she was still dubious about that deeply scooped neckline. Still, it did look nice, and it was rather exhilarating to dress up again so that she looked like an attractive woman instead of an efficient machine. And it just might remind Jim of that fact too.

With her auburn hair brushed out loosely in its natural wave to frame her face, a single strand of pearls around her neck and her best tear-drop earrings, she was ready to go by eight-thirty, when Phil was due to pick her up.

The Talbots' spacious penthouse apartment on Queen Anne Hill was already crowded when they arrived. Through the wide wall of windows on the south side a broad sweeping view was spread out, the lights of the city twinkling in the dark sky. Soft music played in the background, and everyone there was dressed to the teeth.

Phil left Shelley the minute they came inside, scurrying off to spread cheer among the moneyed guests, but she spotted Jim right away. He was standing by the buffet table, looking very handsome with his silvery hair and formal suit. The ubiquitous Vanessa was glued to his side, resplendent in a pink satin creation that looked as though it had cost the earth.

She made her way towards them through the crowd, stopping occasionally to speak to the other guests, and when she reached the table she was at least gratified to see the appreciative look on Jim's face as soon as he saw her. Vanessa, of course, only glared.

'Good evening, Shelley,' Jim said. 'You look very beautiful this evening.'

Their eyes met, and the message he seemed to be sending her warmed her heart. There was gratitude that she'd gone to so much trouble to look her best, but the glint of more intimate appreciation and promise in his soft brown eyes made the whole thing worthwhile.

After greeting her coolly, Vanessa led Jim away as quickly as possible, and Shelley was left standing alone. A white-jacketed waiter passed by just then, his tray laden with drinks. She took a glass of champagne, and turned around to survey the scene.

She spotted Blake Fowler immediately. He was standing in a group of people at the far end of the room by the ornate fireplace, dressed impeccably in evening clothes and inches taller than any of the others, looking as though he'd just stepped down from a movie screen, or out of the pages of a men's fashion magazine.

For a moment, all she could do was stare. He was holding a glass in one hand and gesturing with the other, obviously telling a story, and from the way the three women in the group hung on his every word, their eyes fastened on him with naked hunger, it must have been a good one. Even the men seemed fascinated—quite a feat, since among them Shelley recognised an important lobbyist, the president of the largest local bank and a famous actor.

With one last sweeping gesture, Blake delivered his punch line, and his audience broke into loud appreciative laughter. Shelley watched as he raised his glass to his lips, a bemused expression on his lean face, perfectly at ease and in command, not in the least flustered by all the attention.

Then suddenly he turned his head, and before she could look away his eyes fastened directly on hers, holding them in a direct gaze she couldn't seem to escape. Without altering his expression, he gave her a swift sweeping glance of appraisal.

Then the slashing black eyebrows lifted a fraction of an inch, the corners of his mouth turned up slightly in a rather mocking smile, and in the next instant he had turned back to the group.

Shelley stood there for several seconds, every muscle rigid. She couldn't seem to make herself move. She felt as though she'd been invaded, that those piercing blue eyes had stripped her naked, then entered into her mind, her soul, the very depths of her being.

She gave herself a little shake and took a quick sip of her wine. One last covert glance in Blake's direction revealed only his broad shoulders and the back of his dark head, turned firmly towards her, and she had to smile. Clearly that one penetrating look hadn't made much of an impression on him.

So much for Phil's fairy-tale about the man's interest in her! She wouldn't have to play his shabby game after all. Breathing a silent sigh of relief, she went off to mingle with the crowd.

She knew everyone present quite well, and it wasn't long before she was surrounded by admiring males and glaring wives, chatting easily. The guests had all been carefully selected, made up entirely of Jim's most ardent supporters, and the time passed quickly as she moved from one group to another.

Occasionally during the evening she would catch a glimpse of Blake off in the distance. He always seemed to be surrounded by other people, and made no effort to speak to her. In fact, if he had actively been trying to avoid her, he couldn't have stayed out of her way more successfully.

By ten o'clock she was feeling rather weary of all the talk, the people, the whole scene. The muscles of her face ached from smiling, her feet hurt from the unaccustomed high heels she'd worn to go with the dress, and she was more than ready to leave. Tomorrow would be another busy day, and she had to get some sleep.

She was heading towards Irene Talbot, her hostess, to make her farewell, when out of the corner of her eye she noticed the tall dark man making his way towards her through the crowd. She quickened her step, but wasn't quite fast enough, and before she'd gone far she could sense his presence behind her.

'Good evening,' came his deep, quiet voice.

She turned her head slowly to face him. 'Good evening,' she replied tersely.

'I'm glad to see your embargo on social life doesn't extend to strictly political affairs,' he said easily. 'And to think I almost decided not to come.'

His bright blue eyes swept her up and down. 'I must say it was well worth the effort.'

Shelley knew she was reddening, but couldn't stop herself. 'I'm glad you think so,' she said at last with a tight smile. 'However, I was just leaving myself.'

He cocked an eyebrow at her. 'Oh? Not because of me, I hope.'

'Oh, no, not at all. I'm just tired, and a little bit of this kind of socialising goes a long way with me.'

He nodded. 'I know what you mean.' He put his hand on her arm. 'Come on, then, I'll take you home.'

Once again he was moving way too fast for her, and her first instinct was to pull away from him with a curt refusal. But she'd promised! She looked at him. He was just standing there patiently, as though waiting for her to make up her mind, a slight smile of barely suppressed amusement on his handsome face.

There was something so hypnotic about those blazing blue eyes that Shelley was held by them, almost against her will. And he really was quite a dashing man. Dressed formally, freshly shaven, his dark crisp hair well cut, his spotless white shirt gleaming, he was by far the best-looking man in the room.

Not only had she agreed to co-operate with Phil's battle plan, but traces of lingering resentment at Jim's willingness to go along with the charade made her reckless. If things got out of hand, she could handle it.

'All right,' she said at last. 'Let me just say goodnight to Irene and get my coat.'

Blake dropped his hand from her arm and nodded. 'I'll be waiting for you in the foyer.'

It had started to rain, just a light sprinkling, but enough so that Blake had to use the windscreen-wipers as they drove along the quiet darkened streets.

Although Shelley still had reservations about leaving the party with him, she was glad to escape from the crowded noisy party, and the silence in the smooth powerful car was very relaxing, with only the sound of the tyres swishing on the wet pavement to break the stillness.

Slipping her high-heeled pumps off her aching feet, she wiggled her cramped toes with a sigh of relief. Blake had turned the radio on to her favourite station, one that played mostly old show tunes, and she leaned her head back and closed her eyes.

It wasn't until they reached the centre of town and he made a left turn on to Broadway heading towards Capitol Hill that she was jolted out of the pleasant lethargy. She sat bolt upright and slid her feet back into her shoes.

'Hey,' she said, turning to him, 'I live in the Madrona district, remember?'

He flicked her a quick sideways glance. 'Oh, yes, I remember quite well. But it's early. I thought we might stop for a cup of coffee along the way.' He slowed to a stop at a red light and turned to her. 'Somehow I had the sneaking hunch you weren't planning to invite me in for a cup at your place.'

She had to smile. 'Well, you're right about that,' she replied. 'But I'm not sure coffee is such a good idea at this hour. Doesn't it keep you awake?'

'Nothing keeps me awake,' he told her firmly. He flashed her a wicked grin. 'With one or two exceptions.'

Just then the light turned green, and they moved forward again. 'I thought we'd go to the Dilettante,' he said. 'If you don't want coffee they serve wonderful hot chocolate. Are you hungry? Their desserts are out of this world.'

Shelley wasn't at all sure she liked the way he was simply taking control, masterminding the evening, blithely assuming she'd fall in with his plans. She *was* hungry, however, and the thought of the various exotic—and *rich*—pastries served at the Dilettante was a powerful incentive for her hollow stomach. She hadn't eaten since the cheeseburger she'd had at the office hours ago.

But then he'd pulled up into a parking space, and it was too late to object without creating a scene. Besides, he was already out of the car and coming around to open the door for her. With a resigned shrug, she stepped out on to the pavement beside him. He tucked her arm under his and they walked the half-block to the small restaurant.

Since it was a little too early for the after-theatre crowd, they were seated right away. It was quite warm inside, and after they'd ordered Shelley shrugged out of her coat. When she saw the look on Blake's face, however, she instantly regretted the move. She'd forgotten the low-cut black dress, but he was clearly enjoying it immensely.

He leaned across the tiny table so that his face was only inches away from hers. 'You look like ten million dollars tonight, Shelley,' he said in a low, intimate voice. 'I knew the moment I set eyes on you last night that a gorgeous woman lurked beneath that efficient mask you wear on the job. And I was right.'

Although Shelley was flattered by his words, she couldn't help feeling slightly annoyed at the way he'd expressed them. In typical male fashion he had turned a compliment on her appearance into a pat on the back for his own powers of discernment. Was there no limit to the masculine ego?

'Well, congratulations,' she said in a dry tone. 'That was very clever of you.'

He narrowed his eyes suspiciously at her for a moment, then threw back his head and laughed. Still smiling, strong white teeth flashing against his tanned skin, he leaned back in his chair and gave her a long appreciative look.

'You're rather clever yourself,' he remarked with genuine warmth. 'I like that. Beauty and brains, all in the same delectable package.'

The young waiter arrived with their order just then, and they tucked in with gusto to the rich creamy chocolate torte they'd both decided on. Shelley, no slouch when it came to appetite, was pleased to see that for such a lean, fit man Blake had no more scruples about calories and cholesterol than she herself, and she actually found herself warming to him. Not only was he extremely attractive, but when he dropped his pose of predatory seducer he was fun to be with, actually quite a nice man.

In fact, she was enjoying herself so much that it wasn't until she'd almost finished her torte that she remembered why she was here in the first place.

Quickly she swallowed the last bite, wiped her mouth with her napkin and settled back in her chair.

'That was wonderful, Blake.'

'Glad you enjoyed it. Would you care for another?'

'She held up a hand. 'Please, don't tempt me! No, thank you. I've had more than enough already.' There was a short silence while the waiter refilled their coffee-cups, then, taking a deep breath, Shelley plunged into the icy waters. 'I was wondering,' she began, trying to sound casual, 'if you'd given any more thought to helping Jim with his campaign.'

Blake set his cup back carefully in its saucer, frowned down at it for a second, then raised his eyes to hers again. 'Tell me,' he said, 'how did a nice girl like you get involved in such a dirty game as politics?'

Side-tracked again! 'Oh, it's a long story,' she replied, forcing out a smile. 'And not a very interesting one.'

'Tell me anyway,' he coaxed.

'Well, I went to work for Jim as his secretary when he was practising law. Then when he was elected district attorney I just went along with him.' She laughed. 'Somehow when he decided to run for governor and hired Phil to run his campaign I got promoted to become his assistant.'

'I see. And do you like the work?'

As she thought the question over, it dawned on her that she'd actually never asked it of herself before. She had simply been swept along on her present course by her feelings for Jim, her only real interest what would help him. It had never occurred to her to wonder if she herself was satisfied with the work.

'Well,' she replied carefully at last, 'I'll have to admit it does have its down side. There's a lot of in-fighting in politics, a lot of things that aren't entirely agreeable. But I believe in Jim, and I'll do anything it takes to get him elected.'

'Anything?' he asked in a dead serious tone. 'Do you really mean that?'

She flushed and lowered her eyes. 'No, I guess not,' she said. Then she smiled. 'We all have our limits, don't we? A line we won't cross, no matter what the prize? I'll bet even a hardened newspaperman like you sets boundaries for himself in the pursuit of important stories.'

Blake shrugged. 'Well, that rule doesn't really apply to me. I don't go after the news or write about it—I only manage the paper. My job is to keep it a paying proposition.'

'But you do determine the editorial policy.'

'Not really. Oh, I suppose if there were an issue I cared deeply about I'd probably throw my weight around a little, but I already told you, I'm neutral. It's not that I refuse to support Jim. He's no worse than his opponent. In fact, he's quite possibly a hair better.'

'But you have an obligation!' she rejoined heatedly. 'You owe it to your readers, to the public at large, to try to sway opinion in the right direction.'

He cocked an eyebrow at her. 'And you're convinced your friend Jim is the man to lead the state in the right direction?'

'Of course I am! Otherwise I wouldn't be working for him.'

'Well, I must say your enthusiasm is rather contagious. And you might be right. However, the election is still six weeks off. By then I might change my mind and come out in favour of one or the other.'

'That's fair enough,' she said. She knew she'd wrung the only concession out of him she was likely to get at this point, and she was satisfied.

Blake pushed his chair back and rose to his feet. 'Excuse me for a few minutes,' he said. 'I'll be right back.'

Watching him as he threaded his way around the tables, the graceful way he moved, the self-assured lift to his shoulders in the perfectly tailored formal jacket, not to mention the way every other feminine head in the room turned to follow him as he passed by, Shelley had to wonder why on earth she'd fought Phil so hard about being pleasant to the man.

Not only had she got in her licks about the possibility of Blake's newspaper supporting Jim, but she'd quite enjoyed his company, much more than she'd dreamed possible. It had been such a long time, years actually, since she'd even given a thought to any man but Jim Carruthers that it was quite a satisfying sensation.

As she sat there alone at the table, finishing her coffee, she began to compare them in her mind. Except that they were both successful and extremely good-looking, no two men could have been more different.

There was something so solid about Jim, so reassuring. He made her feel safe. Blake Fowler, on the other hand, was a totally unknown quantity, attractive, of course, even fascinating, but much as a tiger in the jungle might be. She sensed danger in him, and she'd had enough of that in the past to last a lifetime.

When he came back she rose quickly to her feet. 'I really think I'd better be getting home now,' she said. 'It's another gruelling day tomorrow.'

'Whatever you say,' he replied easily.

It wasn't far to her place, and, although the coffee she'd drunk had given her a slight buzz, the prospect of getting home and falling into bed was welcome. When Blake pulled up in front of her building, she turned to him.

'Well, thanks very much for the lift home, Blake. And the dessert.'

She waited a second for him to get out, but when he just sat there, leaning back in his seat, his hands still resting on the steering-wheel, she realised he wasn't going to walk her to the door. With an odd feeling of disappointment, she reached for the handle.

'Shelley,' she heard him say then in a low voice.

She turned around to face him, and once again the blue, blue eyes held her. There was dead silence in the car, and although he made no move towards her she could feel the electric tension building up between them. She opened her mouth to forestall what she knew was coming, but found she couldn't utter a word.

Then he reached out a hand and placed it lightly on her cheek, his eyes still holding hers in the mesmerising blue gaze. His fingers were warm on her skin, the large hand protective rather than threatening, and when his dark head bent towards hers she held her breath, waiting, unable to move a muscle.

His lips were soft and gentle, moving lightly over hers, and as she gave herself up to his kiss he edged closer to her so that their bodies were just touching. The hand on her face moved around to clasp the back of her neck, pulling her closer, and the kiss deepened, became more urgent.

It wasn't until his other arm came around her shoulders and his mouth opened slightly over hers that the first little bell of alarm went off in her head. She pulled back and gazed up at him, wide-eyed. But he wasn't ready to let her go quite yet.

'Oh, Shelley,' he murmured, pressing closer to her.

His mouth claimed hers again. For the life of her she couldn't move, hadn't the will to protest, even when she felt the tip of his tongue on her lips, a hand come around to settle lightly at the base of her throat. The sensations he was arousing in her were too powerful to resist. It was as though some force that had been bottled up in her for ages was suddenly unleashed. Without thinking, acting on pure blind instinct, she raised her hands to run them through the dark crisp hair.

Immediately the hand at her throat slid downwards, his fingers running along the edge of the low-cut neckline, brushing over the bare skin underneath and setting up a tingling sensation all along her spine. Then one hand began to trace the swell of her upper breast, lightly, tentatively, as though waiting for permission to go on. She caught her breath at the sheer pleasure of his touch, but when the hand started to slip lower she suddenly came to her senses.

She pulled away from him, sliding over the seat, and leaned against the door. Nervously she ran a hand through her hair and clutched the openings of her coat together. After a moment or two, her composure somewhat regained, she turned to him.

'I think I'd better go in now, Blake,' she said shakily.

He fastened his gaze on her for one long moment, then nodded, and the next thing she knew he was out of the car, moving towards her side. When he opened the door, she stepped out and they walked slowly together to her front door. Neither of them said a word until she'd fished out her key, unlocked the door and pushed it open.

Then she turned to him again, somehow hoping to undo what had just happened between them. 'Blake . . .' she began.

But he put a finger on her lips, stopping her. 'No,' he said. 'Don't say it. Don't spoil it. It was wonderful.'

'But——'

'I know,' he broke in. His head came down, his lips brushed lightly against hers, and before she could say another word he'd turned and started walking back to the car.

Shelley quickly stumbled inside, closing and locking the door quietly behind her. Then she leaned back against it, in the darkness, listening to him drive away, her head in a whirl.

What was going on here? What had she done? She couldn't think straight, couldn't grasp what had happened to her. The only thing she knew for certain was that her response to his kiss, his touch, had very definitely not been role-playing for Jim's benefit. Far from it!

It suddenly occurred to her that in fact she could be playing a more dangerous game with this man than she'd bargained for. And it had to stop now, before it was too late. She would just have to tell that to Phil tomorrow, and he could take it or leave it.

# CHAPTER THREE

SHELLEY and Phil had small connecting offices at campaign headquarters, mere cubicles actually, since most of the space had to be given over to the many volunteer workers who manned the telephones, sorted the literature, prepared the mailings, and, most important, conducted the opinion polls.

Phil usually showed up quite early, and Shelley was at her desk waiting for him by eight o'clock the next morning, determined to get the issue of Blake Fowler settled once and for all. When she heard him come into his own office, however, she was on the telephone arranging yet another speaking engagement for Jim, and by the time she'd hung up he was already standing in the connecting doorway, a sharp inquisitive look on his face.

'Well?' he said, coming inside and flopping into the chair beside her desk. 'How did it go last night? I assume Fowler took you home. Did you make any progress with him?'

Shelley leaned back in her chair and eyed him carefully. 'That depends on what you mean by progress,' she remarked in a dry tone.

Phil only grinned. 'Why, enlisting his support for Jim, of course. What else?'

'Well, you can forget it,' she said crisply. 'It's not going to work.'

Phil's eyes widened in mock-disbelief. 'I can't believe that. The way you looked last night, surely you must have made some impression on him?'

'Phil, the man isn't interested in the election. He doesn't intend to support either candidate.'

Rising abruptly from her chair, she went over to the tiny window and gazed out at the rain slashing against it for a moment or two to collect her thoughts. Then she turned around to face him.

'Besides, I've been thinking. Since he's so determined to remain neutral about the election, he can't really hurt us, can he? Isn't that good enough?'

Phil's fatuous smirk faded. He crossed his arms over his chest, tilted his chair back and eyed her narrowly.

'Are you trying to tell me you want to give it up?' he asked in a deceptively even tone.

Shelley spread her arms wide. 'Give what up?' she demanded. 'I'm trying to tell you—the man's a stone wall. He has his mind made up that neither candidate is worth supporting, and throwing myself at him won't change it. Your little plan just isn't going to work. He isn't even interested in the election.' She frowned. 'Besides, it goes against the grain to play these games with him.'

He gazed at her thoughtfully for a moment, then said, 'Don't tell me you're falling for the guy.'

'Of course not!' she replied heatedly. 'I just hate the deception, have done from the beginning—you know that.'

Phil gave her one last look, then sighed and rose slowly up out of his chair. 'All right,' he said. 'If you can't stick it, and if neutrality is the best you can get out of him, then I guess we'll have to be satisfied with that.'

Amazed that he'd given in so easily, she could only stare at his retreating figure as he started moving towards his own office. At the door he hesitated, then turned slowly around to face her again, his expression grave.

'It's too bad, though,' he said sorrowfully. 'Even if Fowler does remain neutral, it's still going to be an uphill battle. But if he changes his mind and decides to support Jim's opponent, we're doomed, dead in the water.'

Shelley's mouth flew open, but before she could think of a rebuttal to that argument, which hadn't even occurred to her before, he'd disappeared into his own office, closing the door quietly behind him, getting in the last word, as usual.

Groaning aloud, she sat down at her desk and buried her head in her hands. She'd been all prepared for an argument, threats, a new plan of attack to force her to do his bidding, but that pose of resignation and regretful acceptance simply threw her. The worst of it was, she groaned again, he was right. Jim just might make it if the *News-Tribune* stayed on the fence, but he'd certainly lose if it came out in favour of the other side.

At the moment she wasn't sure she even cared. Why did it all have to be up to her? If Jim couldn't get elected on his own merit, then maybe it was for the best. It wasn't fair! Not only were they expecting her to violate her deepest principles, but were casually throwing her into the arms of a known predator, all for the sake of a stupid election.

Even as she ranted and raved inwardly, however, she knew quite well that there was more to it than that. It wasn't so much that she didn't trust Blake Fowler. After last night, she didn't trust herself. There was a magnetism about the man that made her forget her innate caution where men were concerned, forget the election. Even, she suddenly realised, to forget Jim Carruthers!

But that was unthinkable! She loved Jim, had loved him for years. There was an understanding between them, a tacit one, to be sure, but one she counted on. After the election they would pick up where they'd left off. Vanessa Talbot would be out of the picture then, Jim would be governor...

But would he? What if he was defeated? She believed their relationship would survive that, but if he lost because she refused to do everything in her power to help him she wasn't so sure.

Just then the telephone on her desk shrilled. Grateful for the interruption to her dismal thoughts, she snatched it up on the first ring.

'Carruthers Campaign Headquarters,' she said briskly. 'Shelley Dalton speaking.'

There was a low masculine chuckle. 'My, you sound efficient this morning. You must have slept well last night.'

Speak of the devil! 'Oh,' she said stiffly. 'Good morning, Blake.'

'I was wondering if you'd like to have dinner at my place this evening,' he said smoothly. 'The forecast is for sunshine later in the day, and since I live on the waterfront I thought we might take advantage of the view.'

'I'm sorry,' she replied quickly. 'I promised myself an early evening tonight.'

'But tomorrow's Saturday,' he went on in the same easy tone. 'Don't you ever get a reprieve?'

She laughed shortly. 'Not this close to the election. I'm sorry.'

'Well, I'm sorry too. I was hoping to carry on where we left off last night.'

'What do you mean?' she asked guardedly.

'You know. About the election.'

Although his tone was disarming, apparently guileless, Shelley was still suspicious. 'What about it?'

'Well, I've been thinking over some of the things you said last night. You might be right. Since I'm in a position to sway public opinion, maybe it *is* my obligation to take a stand, regardless of how I feel personally about the candidates.'

'I see,' she said slowly. He *seemed* sincere enough. 'Well, in that case . . .'

'Good,' he said. 'I'll pick you up around seven.'

'No,' she said hastily. 'Tell me where you live and I'll drive myself.'

'All right, if that's what you want.' And he gave her an address in the Blue Ridge district, one of the smartest in the city.

It wasn't until they'd said goodbye and hung up that Shelley realised she'd just agreed to do what she'd sworn she wouldn't, that somehow she'd been out-manoeuvred again.

That evening, as Shelley got ready for her dinner date with Blake, she was still wondering how in the world she'd allowed herself to get into this mess and seriously considering calling Blake and telling him she couldn't make it after all.

All day she'd debated whether to tell Phil about the date, and even now considered calling him to report in. But something held her back. That remark he'd made about falling for Blake still rankled. There was no telling what he'd do if she fed *that* fantasy.

On one thing, however, her mind was firmly made up. There would be no more personal involvement between them. If he sincerely wanted to discuss the election, fine. She'd be doing her part. But it would be strictly business tonight, whether he liked it or not.

To reinforce her stand, she had to dress the part. No more seductive little dresses. She finally decided on a warm brown lightweight suit that effectively muted her high colouring, and arranged her hair in its usual severe style. Glancing in the mirror just before leaving, she was pleased with the remote, touch-me-not image. If it turned him off, so much the better.

Blake's house was a low sprawling structure built out of rough cedar siding and perched high on a bluff overlooking Puget Sound. He'd said it was on the water, so there must be a path winding down to the beach below. The landscaping was muted, with a smooth, well-tended lawn and clusters of rhododendrons and camellias close to the house. An enormous old magnolia tree was placed in the centre of the garden, shading the house from its southern exposure.

Taking a deep breath, she got out of her car, walked up the winding path to the heavy carved oak front door and rang the bell. He appeared almost immediately, as though he'd been waiting for her just on the other side.

If he was startled at the change in her appearance from the very feminine woman back to the efficient machine, he hid it well. Perhaps the blue eyes narrowed just a little as they flicked her up and down, but the broad welcoming smile seemed genuine enough.

'Come in, Shelley,' he said, holding the door open wide and taking her by the arm. 'Right on time—good. I have a real fetish about promptness.'

'Well, so do I,' she replied, laughing. 'In fact, I'm usually at least ten minutes early for every appointment.'

As she stepped inside the wide entrance hall, she was already regretting her choice of clothing and wondering what in the world had possessed her to wear a business suit to an informal dinner. A trouser outfit would have conveyed the no-nonsense image she wanted to project just as well.

Blake himself looked wonderful, dressed in a pair of clean, worn, low-slung jeans, polished loafers and a loose blue knit shirt. He wore casual clothes as well as he did more formal attire, with the same easy air of self-assurance that just bordered on arrogance.

'It's such a warm evening,' he was saying, 'I thought we might have drinks out on the terrace and catch the view. In fact, we could eat out there too if you like. The sunset over the mountains and water is pretty spectacular.'

'Yes,' she agreed, already too warm in her suit, 'I'd like that.'

She followed him into an enormous living-room that was decorated in muted tones of blues and greys with brighter spots of green and yellow in the cushions on the furniture and pictures hanging on the walls. Along one wall was a massive stone fireplace, and in a corner stood a concert grand piano.

'Do you play?' she asked as they passed by.

Blake gave her a rueful smile. 'Let's just say I play *at* it. I'm very fond of music. Later, if you like, I'll play some for you. *Not* on the piano,' he added quickly. 'I have one room given over to a stereo system.'

'All right. I love music too.'

They went through French doors out on to a wide flagstone-paved terrace that commanded a sweeping westerly view of the Sound, the islands across the bay and the further snow-capped peaks of the Olympic mountain range in the distance, the sun lowering behind them.

Shelley stood there for a long moment, savouring the dramatic spectacle, then turned to him. 'It's beautiful, Blake. You're so lucky to live here.'

'Yes,' he replied. 'I know.' He led her over to an upholstered lounge-chair. 'Now why don't you sit down, make yourself comfortable? I have martinis chilling inside.'

He left her then, and as she watched him walking away from her with his long, graceful stride, the confident lift of his broad shoulders, it occurred to her that she really knew very little about him. Somehow she had imagined him in a swinging bachelor pad, and the cool, understated elegance of this beautiful house, the casual clothes, his obvious love of nature, his enjoyment of music, even the piano playing, showed her a side of him she hadn't dreamed existed.

It was as though she was seeing him for the first time as a real human being instead of a predatory womaniser or a political power to be manipulated into helping Jim's campaign. An interesting human being, at that, with depths to his character that weren't at all apparent on that smooth polished surface.

It was quite warm in the still, early evening air, with the glare of the sun reflected off the water, and after a moment Shelley slipped her jacket off and settled back in the padded chair to watch the screeching gulls as they wheeled and dipped along the sandy shore, scavenging for their last meal of the day.

Blake reappeared carrying a tray with a frosty martini pitcher and two fine crystal cocktail glasses. He set the tray down on the redwood table beside her chair, poured out the drinks and handed one to her.

'I hope you like vodka,' he said. 'I can't stand the taste of gin myself.'

'Oh, neither can I,' she replied. She took a taste and smiled up at him. 'These are fine.'

He pulled up a chair across from her and picked up his own glass. They sat there for a moment in silence, sipping their drinks and gazing out at the view.

'Tell me,' she said at last, turning to him, 'how did you get involved in the newspaper business?'

She smiled. 'Struggling young reporter works his way to the top in record time, I'll bet.'

Blake laughed. 'Not exactly. In fact, you couldn't be more wrong. I'm afraid my story isn't that kind of rags-to-riches drama. The *News-Tribune* is part of the family business. We dabble in all sorts of things, but the newspaper was what appealed to me the most. Something about the power of the Press as a force for good struck a chord in me.' He gave her an amused look. 'Disappointed?'

'No, of course not.' She had to wonder just what that 'family business' entailed, but didn't like to ask. It sounded impressive, however. 'Then your family live here in Seattle?'

'Oh, no. The old homestead is in Philadelphia, as a matter of fact. My parents still live in the place I grew up in, along with my two younger brothers. I do have an older married sister living in San Francisco, at least on the same coast, and I see her and her family quite often.'

'That's nice,' she said. 'I'm an only child myself, and I envy you your large family. Although my parents do live closer than yours, in a small town up near the Canadian border, so at least I get to see them often. In fact, my father runs the local newspaper.'

'Well, perhaps you'll have a family of your own one day,' he told her. 'Or are you a dedicated career woman who doesn't want to be tied down to husband, home and children?'

She gave him a suspicious look. It sounded very much as though he was making fun of her, but the expression on his face was merely one of bland curiosity.

'I don't know,' she said. 'I really haven't given it much thought. Right now I just want to get through this campaign in one piece and see Jim elected.'

Even as she spoke the words, it dawned on her that in the hour or so she'd been there she hadn't given Jim's campaign a moment's thought. And that was the only reason she'd come in the first place! She was just about to raise the subject, test the waters to see if he'd meant it when he'd said he'd been thinking it over, when he suddenly rose to his feet.

'I'm starving,' he said. 'How about you? My housekeeper makes a great crab Louis, and it'll just take a second to dish it out and heat up the rolls.'

Without waiting for a reply, he turned on his heel and went back inside the house. She'd missed her chance, but the evening was young. Surely she'd have another one?

After dinner Blake conducted her to what he called his music-room, where he kept an elaborate sophisticated stereo system and large-screen television set. One wall was covered entirely with shelves, with rows of compact discs, videotapes, old-fashioned records and tapes.

Across from the sound system was a long low couch with a marble-topped table in front of it. Blake had made coffee, a delicious rich strong blend, and after they sat down on the couch he poured out two steaming mugs from a silver thermos carafe.

'Now,' he said, moving to switch on the controls, 'what's your pleasure? Show tunes, classical,

country? I have just about everything except hard
rock, which I can't abide.'

'You decide,' she replied, settling back on the
comfortable couch. 'Like you, I enjoy just about
anything.'

She was curious to see what he'd choose, how
he'd read her tastes, and watched him as he stood
there for a moment looking down at her, chin in
hand, a thoughtful expression on his face. There
was only one dim lamp burning low on a table
beside the couch, and its glow cast interesting
shadows over his handsome features.

Finally he went over to the shelves, which seemed
to be very well organised, and after a moment's
search drew out a stack of discs. He crossed over
to the stereo system, fiddled with the switches and
inserted the discs, then came back to sit beside her.

Immediately the room was filled with the lovely
voice of Linda Ronstadt singing love songs from
the Thirties and Forties, slow, sweet, tinged with
melancholy. Surprised at his choice, and inordi-
nately pleased, Shelley turned to him with a smile.

'Was I right?' he asked softly.

'On the button,' she told him with a little laugh.
'It's just what I would have chosen myself. I have
that same recording and play it often.'

Blake nodded with satisfaction. 'I thought so.'

She gave him an enquiring look. 'Really? Why?'

Laughing, he reached out and brushed back a
wisp of hair that had come loose from her bun.
'Somehow I knew that beneath that stern, efficient
exterior beat the heart of a true romantic.'

Then, abruptly, he shifted his lean hips forward,
crossed his long legs on top of the coffee-table,

leaned his head back and closed his eyes. He looked so relaxed that Shelley found her own muscles going limp. She slipped off her shoes and curled her legs under her, giving herself up to the music.

It had been a lovely evening—the beautiful house, spectacular view, fine dinner, good music. Blake was such an easy person to be with, and she'd learned quite a lot about him tonight. He also seemed really interested in her as a person, something she wasn't used to in the rough and tumble of political life where everybody seemed to be using everybody else. She wondered if he'd ever been married, or come close.

She could feel her own eyes closing by the time the record was half over, and at the same time was dimly aware that Blake had moved so close to her that she could feel the rough texture of his jeans against her legs.

'Shelley,' she heard him say in a low voice.

She opened her eyes to see that his face was only inches away, the blue gaze full upon her. When he reached out to take her hand in both of his, large and strong and slightly callused, she started to sit up a little straighter and move away from him, but something held her almost against her will.

'Shelley,' he said again, and as his dark head dipped lower she closed her eyes, knowing what was coming, but unable to resist.

As his mouth found hers, warm and soft and seeking, her heart began to pound erratically. In spite of all her resolutions not to get involved with him, there was something about the romantic setting, about the man himself, that weakened all her defences.

His arms came around her, holding her tight, pulling her closer to him as he twisted his body around to press up against her. His hands were moving on her feverishly now, sliding sensuously over the thin silk of her blouse, and she could feel his quick warm breath on her face, the thudding of his heartbeat next to hers, as his kiss, his embrace, became more urgent.

When his hand settled on her breast, she drew in her breath sharply, but just at that moment the recording came to an end. There was a tiny clicking sound, then silence. It wasn't long before the next disc started to play, but that slight pause was all it took to bring her to her senses, and she pulled back from him, breaking off the kiss.

'Blake,' she said shakily, 'I don't think this is such a good idea.'

He raised his head and gazed down at her. 'I don't see why not.' He ran a hand over her hair, loosening the coil at the back of her neck. 'I like you, Shelley—I like you a lot. I think we could have some good times together.'

She gave a nervous little laugh. 'No doubt,' she said. 'But...'

'Come on now,' he said, cutting her short and reaching for her again. 'Relax.'

By now, however, the spell was broken, and this time when she pulled away from him she slid off the couch and jumped to her feet. She stood there for a moment, straightening her clothing and pinning her hair in place, unable to look at him. What was there about this man that, in spite of all her good intentions, she seemed to end up in his arms every time they met?

'Shelley?' he said at last, puzzled. 'What is it?'

She turned around and gave him a bright smile. 'If you'll recall, the reason I came over here tonight in the first place was because you said you wanted to discuss the possibility that your newspaper would support Jim.'

He leaned back and crossed his arms over his chest. 'That's right, but that's no reason——'

'Well?' she broke in quickly before he could go on. 'Don't you think that's what we'd better do?' She glanced down at the table. 'In fact, I'd like another cup of coffee if it's still hot.'

'Certainly,' he said.

He reached for the thermos carafe, unscrewed it, and poured out a cup for her. 'So,' he said, holding it out, 'let's discuss.'

She took the cup from him and sat down on the edge of the couch, as far away from him as she could get. She took a few sips to give herself time to collect her thoughts, uncomfortably aware that his eyes were fixed on her every second, then set the cup down and turned to him.

'Well, first of all,' she began hesitantly, 'I'd like to know what you have against him. I mean, you said yourself his opponent was no better.' She laughed. 'A rather backhanded compliment, I admit, but it did give me a little hope.'

Blake leaned forward, long legs apart, his elbows braced on his knees, and stared thoughtfully into the distance for some time. The music was a lush rendition of waltzes, heavy on the strings, and in its own way as romantic as the Ronstadt songs, but she wasn't going to fall into *that* trap again.

She sat there quietly, waiting for him to speak, watching him. His features were in profile and he was frowning slightly. With his dark hair tousled from their recent encounter, one stray lock falling over his forehead, he looked quite boyish—and even more devastatingly attractive.

'All right,' he said at last, turning to her, 'I'll tell you what I have against Jim Carruthers.' He held up a hand and began ticking off on his fingers. 'Number one, he's an opportunist, but then so is his opponent. Number two, his programmes are so stale, so trite, they would have served just as well fifty years ago. He doesn't even begin to address the real problems in the state today.'

He began to enumerate several, from ecology to the faltering timber industry, the homeless, the plight of the farmers, the shambles of the education system, the soaring cost of medical care, until Shelley held up a hand to stop him.

'All right, all right,' she said. 'You've made your point. I know how important those issues are, and I also know Jim hasn't had much to say in the way of specific solutions. But don't you see? If he comes out too strongly on one side or the other, he'd be certain to lose a critical segment of the vote.'

'I see only too well,' was the dry response. 'So, instead of a positive programme, he tries to please everybody.' He shook his head. 'Can't be done, I'm afraid.'

'Listen,' she said earnestly, leaning forward to gaze into his eyes. 'I happen to know what Jim stands for, and I promise you you'd agree with every plan he has. But first he has to get elected. He can't do that if he alienates half the voters.'

'Oh, Shelley, that excuse is as old as politics itself. I'm sure Julius Caesar said the same thing when he decided to make himself emperor of Rome. Remember? Bread and circuses. And it's exactly how Hitler came to power.'

'Perhaps,' she replied grudgingly. 'But there's one important difference.'

'Oh. And what's that?'

'The fact that Jim Carruthers is an honourable man. I know him, Blake. He really cares about good government. He's a man of the highest integrity, the finest moral principles.'

He didn't say anything for several moments, just sat gazing at a point beyond her head, not quite focusing on her face. Finally he heaved a deep sigh, poured himself a cup of coffee and took a long swallow. Then he turned to her again, his expression quite solemn.

'You're in love with him, aren't you?' he stated flatly.

It was the last thing she had expected him to say, and she was so flustered she couldn't think how to answer him. She hated being pinned down like that where she either had to lie or admit to a fact she was trying to hide.

Before she could come up with a reply, however, he'd started speaking to her again. 'You've gone on at some length about Jim's fine qualities. Now you tell me—do you really think it's so honourable the way he's using Vanessa Talbot?'

'He's not using her,' she snapped back immediately. 'The Talbots are supporting him because they believe in him.'

He raised one heavy dark eyebrow. 'Oh? That isn't the impression I get, and I'm quite certain Vanessa doesn't believe it for a minute either. I'd bet my bottom dollar he's made her promises just the way he has the voters, promises he's either going to break once he's elected——' he broke off for a second to fix her with a steady blue gaze '—or keep, in which case you'll be the loser.'

Everything in Shelley rebelled against his interpretation of the relationship between Jim and Vanessa, but in her heart she had to admit it made sense. What was more, it was exactly what she'd been afraid of all along, only she hadn't wanted to face it. Vanessa obviously expected their personal relationship to continue after the election. If it did, then that meant Jim's promises to Shelley herself, however tacit, would be broken. If it didn't, then Blake was right. He'd just been using Vanessa.

'I told you once,' Blake was saying softly now, 'that politics was a dirty game. I'm sorry, but that's just the way it is. I can't even really blame Carruthers. Under our system, a man has to compromise his principles just to get elected at all.'

Shelley was so confused by now that she didn't know what to say. She just wanted to block everything he'd said out of her mind. What did he know? He was only a jaded, cynical man who couldn't see real integrity when it came up and hit him over the head.

'I see,' she said tightly, rising to her feet and looking down at him. 'You paint a pretty bleak picture.'

He got up to stand beside her, gazing at her with something like pity in his eyes. 'It *is* a bleak picture.

The real reason I haven't supported either candidate is because I don't trust any politician. All I'm saying to you now is that neither should you. You'll only get hurt.'

'And I suppose I should trust you!' she rejoined hotly.

He laughed. 'But I never asked you to trust me. I don't make promises to women I have no intention of fulfilling.'

What she wanted to do was slap that self-satisfied smile off his face, but she stopped the impulse just in time. She didn't care what he said about Jim. She believed in him; she always had. And faith in a person meant trusting him or her. She had no choice. And it wouldn't help him to antagonise Blake Fowler.

'Well,' she said, 'I can see that my trip here was all for nothing.' She forced out a smile. 'But I had to try.'

'Oh, I wouldn't say it was a total waste,' he commented. 'I had a wonderful time.'

She clamped her back teeth together to keep from making a stinging retort and smiled again. 'That wasn't quite what I meant.'

'Well, I haven't said I wouldn't support your hero, have I?'

Hope rose within her. 'You mean ... ?'

Blake held up a hand. 'I mean only what I say. The election is still a few weeks off. There's still plenty of time to change my mind.'

'Well, I guess I'll just have to be satisfied with that. Now I think I'd better be on my way.'

After she had collected her jacket and handbag, he walked her to her car. There was a bright moon shining above, with only a few wispy clouds floating by in the late night breeze. The air had turned a little chilly, but at least it wasn't raining.

'Well, thanks for the meal,' she said when they reached her car. 'It was great. And the music.'

'My pleasure,' he said, opening the door for her. Before she could get inside, however, he put a hand on her arm, holding her back. 'I'd like to see you again, Shelley,' he said in a low voice. 'I know how you feel about Carruthers, but I'm not asking for a lifetime commitment, you know. That wouldn't suit me any more than it would you. And I meant it when I said I thought we could have a good time together.'

Before she could reply, he had clasped her around the neck and bent down to kiss her firmly on the mouth. After all that had passed between them that evening, she was so surprised at the sudden gesture that she didn't think to resist.

He let her go after only a few seconds, and she slid quickly inside the car, closed the door and started the engine. As she started down the driveway, the back of her neck was still prickling from the sensations his last kiss had aroused in her. She also had the distinct feeling that he was still standing there watching her every inch of the way.

## CHAPTER FOUR

THE next morning as she sat in her small kitchen eating breakfast, Shelley was still mulling over the evening before, especially the conversation with Blake. There was a lot of truth in what he'd said. Politics *was* a dirty business, and, much as she hated to admit it, Jim Carruthers was right in the thick of it.

But it was Blake himself and her own reaction to him that puzzled her most. He was obviously a man who put his own pleasure first in his life, and much of that pleasure seemed to centre on women. Yet, in his way, he had a code of honour that might not be the most admirable in the world, but did have its own integrity. He had said he didn't make promises he had no intention of fulfilling, and she believed him. Although he claimed he wanted to enjoy what he called a 'good time' with her, he had made it crystal-clear that he was making no commitments or promises.

She also had to admit that in spite of everything she was attracted to him. Not in love with him or anything like that, of course. But while she was waiting around for Jim to get elected so that they could pick up where they'd left off it was flattering to be sought after by such a dashing man as Blake Fowler. He'd said he wanted to see her again. Did she dare? He seemed to wield a blatant sexual power that was hard to resist, and that could be dangerous.

She had just stepped out of the shower and was drying off when the telephone rang. Slipping on a terry-cloth robe, she padded barefoot into the kitchen to answer it.

It was Phil, his voice throbbing with excitement. 'Have you seen the *News-Tribune* this morning?' he barked.

'No. Not yet. Why?'

'Well, go get it and cast your lovely green eyes over the lead editorial, then call me back. I'm at home.'

With that, he hung up. Shelley stood there for a moment, the dial tone buzzing in her ear, wondering what in the world had given Phil such a jolt so early in the morning. Then she set the receiver down and ran to the front door, where the morning paper was lying on the mat as usual. She snatched it up and carried it back to the kitchen.

As she leafed quickly to the editorial page, her eye was caught immediately by the bold-faced headline: NEWS-TRIBUNE ENDORSES CARRUTHERS FOR GOVERNOR.

She sank slowly down in her chair and began to read.

While this newspaper cannot in conscience whole-heartedly support either candidate, we feel it our public duty to give an informed opinion to our readers. Therefore the publishers of the *News-Tribune* have decided to endorse James D. Carruthers as next Governor.

There was just one more short paragraph outlining Jim's career as practising lawyer and his present post as district attorney, with emphasis on his very real accomplishments. After she'd finished reading, she got up and poured herself a cup of coffee, then carried it over to the window and stared out at the falling rain, still stunned, her mind in a turmoil.

Of course she was pleased that Blake had decided to support Jim after all, even if the wording was a rather backhanded compliment. But something was wrong, and she couldn't quite put her finger on what it was.

In her work she'd had to deal closely with reporters, and in the process had gained some knowledge of how newspapers functioned. Morning editions were 'put to bed'—that was, set in type, late the previous night. But the actual copy had to be in the hands of the layout people long before it went to the printer.

She'd arrived at Blake's house at seven o'clock, and he certainly hadn't written the editorial while she was there. And by the time she left it would have been too late to get it in the morning edition. So it had to have been written and submitted long before she got there. And *that* meant he'd already decided to support Jim before the tender little love scene in his music-room.

A cold anger started to rise up in her. The cup slipped from her hand and smashed on the floor. He'd *used* her! Deceived her! He'd known all along he was going to endorse Jim, and had only kept her guessing, played coy, held out the possibility as a carrot, just to try to lure her into bed.

'The rat!' she said aloud. 'The unspeakable rotter!'

She had to talk to Phil. Trembling now from head to foot with a white-hot rage, she stumbled to the telephone and with fumbling fingers dialled Phil's number. As it rang, she took deep breaths to calm herself, and by the time he answered she felt more in control.

'Hi, Phil,' she said. 'It's me.'

'Well?' he crowed. 'Aren't you the clever one! My heartiest congratulations. You did it! Didn't I say you could?'

She hardly knew how to answer. Clearly he'd already jumped to the conclusion that it was her influence that had changed Blake's mind, probably that she'd actually gone to bed with him. But if she told him the truth, that she hadn't had the slightest effect on his decision, he wouldn't believe her anyway.

'Well, I don't really think I had much to do with it,' she finally hedged. 'But this will certainly help.'

'Help!' he shouted in her ear. 'It'll put Jim so far over the top the other side'll never catch up. By the way,' he went on in a more subdued confidential tone, 'Jim is extremely pleased. He'll probably call you some time today to thank you personally, but he asked me to pass along his gratitude.' He chuckled. 'You really did perform above and beyond the call of duty this time, Shelley. I'm proud of you.'

'Phil,' she tried again, 'I really didn't do anything—you've got to believe me.'

The last thing she wanted was for Jim to think she'd actually slept with Blake Fowler just to help get him elected. She'd have to talk to him, tell him it wasn't true, no matter what Phil thought.

'Oh, I believe you,' Phil said. 'In fact I knew yesterday morning what Fowler was going to do.'

'Yesterday morning?' she asked in a small voice. 'But how?'

'Ah, I have a spy on the *News-Tribune* who keeps me informed.'

Once again anger rose up in her like a white-hot flame. 'Then why all the folderol about my seducing him?' she asked furiously.

'Shelley, we never asked you to seduce the man, only to try and influence him. Besides, I only found out yesterday what he was going to do. As far as I knew we still needed your help.' He paused for a moment. 'Er—it didn't go that far, I take it?'

'No!' she snapped. 'But you could have told me sooner.'

She finally managed to get rid of Phil, and was about to dial Jim's private number when the telephone jangled again. It must be him! she thought, and snatched it up.

But it wasn't Jim. 'Good morning,' came Blake's familiar cool masculine voice. 'Have you seen the morning paper?'

For a moment Shelley couldn't speak. She kept opening and closing her mouth, just like a fish gasping for air, trying to think of some wounding accusation, but nothing really clever came to her.

'You've got some nerve, calling me,' she finally bit out.

'Why?' He sounded genuinely bewildered. 'I thought you'd be pleased. It's what you wanted, isn't it?'

'You deceived me!' she spluttered. 'You made me think you hadn't decided what to do when all along you knew quite well.'

There was a short silence. 'Well, now,' he said easily, 'isn't that a little like the pot calling the kettle black?'

'I don't know what you mean,' she replied stiffly.

'Sure you do—you're not stupid. I told you politics was a dirty game. Weren't you using me to get support for your hero? And now that you've learned I was going to support him anyway, you feel you've been deceived. I was only playing by your rules, Shelley.'

By now her cheeks were burning and she felt faint, with anger still, but also with a growing sense of shame at her own part in the shoddy charade. All she wanted now was to get off the telephone so that she could go and lick her wounds in peace and salvage what little self-respect she had left. But before she did she had to make a stab at getting in the last word.

'Well, all I can say,' she stated flatly, 'is that you must be pretty hard up for female companionship if you have to resort to tricking women into bed.'

'Hold on now,' he protested. 'It wasn't like that!'

'Oh, no?' she enquired loftily. 'How do you figure that?'

To her chagrin, he started chuckling deep in his throat. 'Well, for one thing,' he said, still laughing, 'in spite of my best efforts it didn't end up like that, did it?'

'No!' she cried, furious at his amusement—at *her* expense. 'Believe me, there was never any danger of that, thank God!'

With that, she slammed down the receiver and started pacing up and down the tiny kitchen, wringing her hands and muttering to herself. The worst of it was, he was right! He *had* been playing by her rules. Or Phil's rules, to be more accurate. And Jim's! But that thought was too painful to bear thinking about. She had to talk to him, get the whole thing straightened out.

She glanced at her watch. It was just past ten o'clock. With luck he'd be in his office, catching up on his regular work. There was no point in calling him—he wouldn't answer. She'd just have to go down there in person and hope he'd be there.

The district attorney's office was located in the administration building, an ugly concrete structure not far from the court-house. It was virtually deserted on Saturday morning, and Shelley's footsteps echoed hollowly on the tiled floor as she made her way to Jim's office.

When she stepped inside, she could hear him speaking on the telephone. With a sigh of relief, she went over to his door. When he looked up and saw her he raised his eyebrows, smiled, beckoned her inside and motioned her to the chair across him.

She sat down to wait while he finished his conversation, and gazed around the room. As her eye fell on each familiar object, the rows of legal tomes on the shelves, the large globe in the corner, the diplomas on the wall, she wished from the bottom of her heart that Jim had never decided to run for governor.

She'd been so happy here! She'd loved working for him. The cases he handled were so interesting that she'd looked forward to every day at work.

Now that was all over. Not only was she no longer his secretary, his indispensable right hand, as he used to call her, but she'd become embroiled in a sordid game that threatened to spoil her whole relationship with the man she'd loved for so long.

'Well,' he said at last, hanging up the telephone, 'am I glad to see you! In fact, I was just going to call you.'

'Actually, Jim, there's something I need to talk to you about, too, and I was hoping you'd be here.'

'First,' he said, 'I want to thank you for the splendid job you did with Blake Fowler. You probably won me the election.'

'But that's just what I wanted to talk to you about,' she said, straining forward eagerly. 'I didn't *do* anything. I mean . . .' She hesitated, flustered, then shrugged helplessly, unable to go on.

Jim chuckled deep in his throat. 'Now, Shelley, don't be so modest. Phil and I both could see that you had the man well-hooked right from the beginning.' His resonant voice faded to a lower, more confidential tone. 'Now, I know you weren't particularly thrilled about what Phil wanted you to do, but . . .'

'But that's just it!' she cried, jumping to her feet. She braced her hands on the edge of his desk and leaned over it, gazing earnestly down at him. 'It's what I've been trying to tell you. Blake's decision to support you had nothing to do with me.'

He gazed up at her thoughtfully. 'All right,' he said quietly at last, 'if you say so. But I can't see what difference it makes. Whatever the reason, we got what we wanted from him, and I can't believe you had nothing to do with it.'

'Can't you see?' she groaned, desperate now to make him understand. 'It makes *all* the difference! I couldn't bear to have you think I . . .' She felt the hot tears stinging behind her eyes and turned away.

'Shelley, Shelley,' he said, rising from his chair and coming up behind her, his hands on her shoulders. 'How could you imagine I would ever think anything derogatory about you? Come on now, pull yourself together. We should be celebrating, not weeping.'

She took a deep breath and turned around to face him. When she saw the look of concern on his face, she knew it was going to be all right. He did understand. Hastily she brushed the back of her hand over her eyes and gave him a tremulous smile.

'I was so afraid you'd get the wrong idea,' she said, her voice still a little shaky.

He put his arm around her shoulders and gave her a warm hug. 'This whole thing has been a strain on all of us,' he said warmly. 'But soon it will all be over, just a few more weeks. Then . . .' His voice trailed off, but the promise in his voice was unmistakable.

Then what? she wanted to ask him. Did she dare try to pin him down? She desperately needed some reassurance from him, not only that he understood about Blake, but that when the election was over he and she would pursue their own personal relationship without the encumbrance of Talbots *or* Fowlers.

As though able to read her mind, Jim bent down to peck her lightly on the cheek. 'You do understand, don't you, Shelley, that until the election is over my personal life has to be put on hold?'

She nodded. 'Of course.'

'Now,' he said, 'that's settled, and we won't need to bother about it ever again.'

He dropped his hand from her shoulders and went back to his desk. Watching him as he picked up the telephone and started dialling again, Shelley had the distinct impression that she was being dismissed. What she wanted was for him to ask her to stay, tell her he needed her help with something, ask her to have lunch with him.

But she knew he wasn't going to do any of those things. And even though she was somewhat reassured she really didn't wholly understand why it had to be that way. He'd said his personal life had to be put on hold, but clearly that did not include Vanessa Talbot.

Feeling somewhat like a dog who had just been thrown a bone, she gave him a little wave, turned around and left.

She had taken the bus into the city, always slow on Saturdays, and by the time she got off at her stop it was past noon. She walked slowly the half-block to her building, still pondering the conversation with Jim. She wasn't in the least satisfied with the way it had gone, but apparently she'd have to be for now.

She was so absorbed in her own thoughts that she didn't notice the man get out of the dark Mercedes parked at the kerb in front of her apartment until she almost bumped into him. When she looked up, startled, it was to see Blake grinning down at her.

'Careful,' he said, grabbing her arm to steady her. 'You could hurt someone that way.'

'What are you doing here?' she asked.

'I came to take you to lunch.'

'No, thank you,' she snapped. She pulled her arm out of his grasp, turned around and started walking away from him.

'Hey,' he called, moving into step beside her. 'Don't be like that.' He put his hand on her arm, lightly this time, stopping her. 'We need to talk,' he went on in a low voice.

Shelley turned to him with a sigh. 'We have nothing to talk about. You did what you had to do, and since it's what I wanted in the first place we should both be happy.'

He grinned at her. 'Well, maybe you got what you wanted, but I sure as hell didn't! Come on now, be a sport. There's a nice little café around the corner—you won't even have to get in my car. After all, since you came out the winner in our little game, you can afford to be as gracious in your victory as I am in my defeat.'

She eyed him suspiciously. He was having her on, she knew that quite well, but there was something about the way he was looking at her that made her soften towards him. And he was right, after all. She had won, while he'd actually gained nothing.

'Oh, all right,' she said at last. 'I guess it wouldn't hurt anything to have lunch.'

'My, your graciousness overwhelms me,' he commented drily.

They went around the corner to the small café, a tiny place that specialised in Greek food, with bare floors and small tables set close together along the narrow walls. A bouncy young waitress with dark flashing eyes seated them, and they both ordered moussaka.

When the girl left, swishing her hips a little, clearly for Blake's benefit, he settled back in his chair and fastened his eyes on Shelley, the blazing blue so intense she almost couldn't meet them.

'Now,' he said, 'I want to explain about——'

'There's no need to explain,' she broke in hurriedly. 'You said it yourself. Politics is a dirty game.'

'Will you please quit interrupting me when I'm trying to be humble?' he asked in exasperation. 'That doesn't happen often, and you should feel flattered. Now, I admit I strung you along when I'd planned all the time to support Jim, but doesn't it mean anything that I was attracted to you and simply wanted to get to know you better? That just seemed like the only way at the time.' He shrugged. 'Perhaps not the noblest of motives, but I suspected right from the beginning that one of the reasons you agreed to see me at all was to further the career of your hero. You can't deny that.'

Shelley gave him a wry smile. 'Well, I'll have to admit that my hands weren't entirely lily-white in the whole affair. I did hope to persuade you to give Jim your support.'

He gave her a look of mock-astonishment. 'You mean to tell me you weren't bowled over by my charms?'

She laughed. 'Well, that too, of course. Let's just call it a draw.'

He shook his head slowly. 'Hardly that. As I said when I called you this morning, you got what you wanted. I didn't.'

The piercing blue eyes bored into her, and she looked away, flustered. 'I'm afraid I can't help that,' she mumbled.

The waitress came back just then with their order. Grateful for the interruption, and actually quite hungry, Shelley immediately picked up her fork and tucked in, hoping he'd drop the subject.

But he obviously had other ideas. 'But you can,' he said.

She glanced up at him. 'Can what?'

'You can help it.'

'How?'

'Simple. Have dinner with me tonight.'

She stared at him. 'I can't do that.'

'I don't see why not,' he returned in a reasonable tone.

She waved her fork in the air. 'Well, what else has this whole thing been all about? I mean, after what's happened, I don't see that we have a basis for any kind of meaningful relationship.'

He chewed silently for a moment, then swallowed and took a long drink of water. 'Are you trying to tell me you're not attracted to me?' he asked. 'Because if you are,' he went on before she had a chance to open her mouth, 'I don't believe you.' He leaned across the table so that his face was only inches away from hers, his voice low and intimate. 'I may be a confirmed bachelor, but I haven't lived like a monk all these years, and I know quite well by now when a woman is really responding and when she's just pretending.' He leaned back again. 'And lady, you weren't pretending.'

Shelley's face went up in flame. 'All right,' she said at last in a grudging tone. 'So I'll admit you

caught me off guard a few times with your wining
and dining and music, but that doesn't mean it's
going to happen again.'

He cocked his head to one side and eyed her
silently for a few seconds, as though trying to read
her thoughts. 'What are you afraid of, Shelley?' he
asked at last in a deceptively soft voice. 'Is it me?
Or is it yourself?'

'Don't be ridiculous!' she spluttered. 'I'm not
afraid of anything. I just don't see the point of
getting involved. You certainly aren't interested in
anything serious or committed, and I'm——' She
broke off, realising she'd already said too much.

But he wasn't going to let her off that easily.
'You're still hung up on Jim Carruthers, aren't
you?' he asked quietly. He shook his head. 'My
God, Shelley, haven't you realised by now that he's
only using you? I don't understand how such a
smart girl can be so blind.' He shrugged. 'Of course,
he's only using Vanessa Talbot too, but if any
woman is going to win the prize it'll be Vanessa.
I'll give you any odds you care to make on that.'

Really stung by his words, Shelley sat up ramrod-
straight and raised her chin at him. 'I don't intend
to discuss that subject,' she stated firmly. 'Not with
you or anyone else.'

'All right,' he said with a lift of his broad
shoulders, 'have it your way.'

They continued to eat in silence then, but by now
Shelley had lost her appetite and only pushed her
food around her plate. He was having no trouble
in that department, however, and when he'd finished every last bite he leaned his head back and
gazed thoughtfully into space for some moments.

'So,' he said at last, 'you won't have dinner with me tonight? You're firm on that?'

'Yes,' she replied, wiping her mouth with the napkin then setting it down beside her plate. 'I'm afraid so.'

He nodded. 'All right. I told you I was attracted to you, that I thought we could have some good times together, and my impression was that you were attracted to me too. Apparently I was wrong, and since the one thing I won't do is beg I won't bother you again.' He smiled at her to take the sting out of his words. 'However, since we'll probably be running into each other from time to time, there's no reason why we can't be friends, is there?'

Shelley eyed him carefully. 'No,' she replied slowly. 'If you really mean it.'

He laughed. 'Oh, I do, believe me. I know when to give up a lost cause.'

'And no more playing games,' she added with feeling.

Blake leaned back in his chair and gave her a long look. 'Just what makes you so certain I've been playing games?'

'Well?' she demanded, making a sweeping gesture with her hand. 'Haven't you? What else would you call——?'

'Now hold on, just a minute,' he broke in, his voice steely. 'Just keep quiet and listen to me for one minute. Now,' he went on in a softer tone, 'try and get this through your head. As delightful as the prospect of getting you into my bed might be, I'm not playing games with you. There's more to it than that. I really do care about you, Shelley, and I could learn to care a lot more. But I won't play second fiddle to some damned politician.'

He seemed sincere enough, and for a moment Shelley felt herself weakening towards him. But there was still something about him she didn't quite trust. Besides, she was already committed to Jim. Nothing could change that.

'All right,' she said at last. 'I'm sorry.'

'As well you should be,' he commented sanctimoniously. He held up a hand for the waitress. 'Now, how about some dessert?'

'Oh, I don't know, I'm pretty full.'

The waitress came scurrying over, pad in hand, as though she'd only been waiting for his summons. Blake flashed her a smile, and Shelley could see her visibly melting. She herself might just as well not have been there. There was no denying the man's magnetism, and she congratulated herself once again that she was immune to it.

'I'll have a slice of baklava,' he said to the girl, 'and a cup of coffee.' He looked at Shelley. 'How about you?'

'All right, I'll give it a try.'

When the waitress was gone, he braced his elbows on the table and laced his long fingers together. 'How old are you, Shelley?' he asked out of the blue.

She was so taken aback by the direct question that she didn't think to evade it. 'Twenty-seven,' she replied.

'Hmm,' he murmured. 'A few years older than I thought. And how long have you worked for Jim?'

'Four years, counting the time I was his secretary.'

'And you've never been married?'

She reddened. 'Well, as a matter of fact, I have.'

He raised his eyebrows at that. 'Really? I never would have guessed. There's a rather virginal quality about you that made me doubt it. What happened?'

She frowned. 'I'd really rather not talk about it.'

'Oh, come on. We're friends, remember? I mean, just because it has to stop there it doesn't mean I don't like you or am not interested in you. Just as a friend, of course.'

She gave him a suspicious look. It sounded very much as though he was making fun of her again, but his expression was guileless enough.

'Well, it's actually a pretty trite story,' she said slowly. 'I was very young and impressionable. He was a few years older and seemed quite dashing.' She gave a wry little laugh. 'The only problem was he felt duty bound to pass his charms around rather indiscriminately—almost,' she added drily, 'from our honeymoon.'

'Ah,' he said. 'Like that, was it?'

'Oh, yes,' she replied, warming to the subject. 'He was handsome, charming, successful, every girl's dream. And totally undependable, as slippery as an eel, with no more concept of the meaning of commitment than a two-year-old.'

She hadn't thought about David for years. After their divorce he'd disappeared out of her life, gone to Australia someone had said, and she'd never heard from him again. What a charmer he'd been! In fact, she realised suddenly, a man very much like Blake Fowler, and it was on the tip of her tongue to tell him so, but just then their coffee and dessert arrived.

'Well,' Blake said, between bites, 'that explains it.'

'Explains what?'

'Why you're afraid to risk getting hurt again, why you're so caught up in this hero-worship of a man old enough to be your father. But the irony is that you can get just as hurt playing it safe as you can taking a chance.'

She gave him a long withering look. 'That's your diagnosis, is it, Dr Fowler?' she asked in a biting tone. 'You've got it all figured out.' She leaned towards him and fixed him with a gimlet stare. 'And how do you diagnose your own case? You and all the men like you, pursuing anything reasonably attractive in skirts as a sort of trophy, terrified of commitment.'

His face hardened. 'You don't know what you're talking about,' he growled ominously.

Delighted to see that she'd struck a nerve, Shelley pressed on. 'Oh, I see! It's all right for you to pry your way into every nook and cranny of *my* psyche and come to your half-baked conclusions, but when the shoe's on the other foot it pinches and you back off.' She rose to her feet. 'I have to be going. Thanks for the lunch.'

'You haven't finished your baklava,' he protested.

'You finish it!' she snarled, and walked away from the table. 'And I hope you choke on it,' she muttered to herself as she went.

Back at her apartment, Shelley immediately changed into an old pair of blue jeans and worn cotton shirt and embarked on a manic house-cleaning spree. At this point she was so sick of politics that entire governments could fall and she wouldn't care.

She was even more sick of men. Of Jim and his mealy-mouthed kowtowing to the Talbots, of Phil and his demonic machinations, and most of all of Blake Fowler and his stupid diagnosis of her personal situation. What was so wonderful about his life that he could probe into hers so blithely?

'Afraid of getting hurt, indeed!' she muttered aloud as she jabbed the vacuum cleaner viciously into every nook and cranny of the small apartment. 'He's one to talk!'

Finally, by four o'clock, exhausted and dripping with perspiration, she'd had enough. The hard physical labour had done her good, however, and she surveyed the spotless rooms with satisfaction. Even her junk drawer was in order, for the first time in months.

After a long, leisurely soak in a hot tub, she put on an old comfortable robe, wrapped a towel around her wet head and went into the kitchen to make herself a cup of tea. She debated finishing the slice of sweet roll left from breakfast, but the half-eaten moussaka was still churning in her stomach, and she wasn't really hungry.

As she sat at the small table by the kitchen window drinking her tea and gazing out at the gathering dusk, she felt a sudden urge to call her parents. It had been a long time since she'd spoken to them, and, although she knew they understood how frantic these last weeks before the election could be, an unpleasant feeling of guilt nagged at her for her neglect.

Besides, she missed them, needed to hear their voices again. She was their only child, born when they were both past forty, and the three of them were a close-knit little family. In fact, when Shelley finished college her father had wanted her to work for him on his newspaper, but by then she'd met David and embarked on that travesty.

Her mother answered the telephone, her familiar voice like a breath of fresh air in Shelley's ear.

'Hello, Mother,' she said. 'It's your prodigal daughter.'

'Oh, darling, we were just talking about you. How have you been? Terribly busy, I'm sure.'

'Afraid so. Anyway, I'm fine—just a little tired, but it'll all be over soon. How about you and Dad?'

There was a slight hesitation, and all Shelley's instincts were alerted. Something was wrong, but she knew her mother well enough to realise that it wouldn't do any good to press her.

'Well, to tell you the truth, dear,' her mother finally replied, 'your father had a rather nasty turn a few weeks ago. Seems his heart isn't what it used to be, and he's going to have to start taking it a little easier.'

Icy fingers of fear ran up and down Shelley's spine. 'Mother!' she cried. 'Why didn't you tell me?'

'Now don't upset yourself. I didn't want to worry you for nothing, so I waited until we knew how things stood. As a matter of fact I was thinking about calling you tonight to tell you about it. So long as he takes care of himself, he'll be fine.'

'What does that mean?' Shelley demanded. 'Is he in the hospital?'

'Oh, heavens no. He's not even in bed. He just can't do all the things he's used to doing. Dr Evans and I are both trying to talk him into giving up the paper, but you know how stubborn he is. Perhaps after the election you might be able to come up for a short visit and help me convince him to retire.'

'Yes, of course I will—I'd planned on it. I'll come right now if you want me to.'

'No, dear, no need for that. I know how important this election is to you, and there's no emergency.' Her mother chuckled softly. 'I have a suspicion he's more frightened about what happened than he likes to let on, so he pretty much confines his activities to the paper, and I've hired someone to do the heavy work around the house.'

'Well, in just a few more weeks the election will be over, and the first thing on my agenda is coming home for a nice long visit.'

They discussed the campaign and Shelley's high hopes for the outcome for a few more minutes, then said goodbye. After she'd hung up, she stood there for a moment, frowning down at the telephone. In spite of her mother's reassurances, she was filled with a sickening feeling of dread about her father. What if she were to lose him?

# CHAPTER FIVE

ONE bright sunny morning, a few weeks later, Shelley was getting ready for the weekly policy meeting with Jim and Phil, and as usual wondering what to wear. Seattle had been enjoying a spell of unseasonably warm weather, and she'd already put away most of her summer things.

She had just about decided on a lightweight cotton suit when the telephone rang. It was Phil, calling to tell her the meeting place had been changed from the office to the local tennis club.

'Why the tennis club?' she asked.

'Actually, it was my idea. Jim's been feeling frazzled lately with all the last-minute campaigning, and I thought a good hard game of tennis might brace him up. And he's an excellent player.'

'Good idea,' she replied. 'What time shall I meet you?'

'Well, he doesn't have a firm date with anyone, just figured he'd pick up whoever was looking for a game. Why don't you plan to meet me there in an hour, and we'll just play it by ear?'

After they'd hung up, Shelley went to the bedroom, put the suit back in the wardrobe and took out a flowered sundress. If she was going to spend the fine morning lolling around the posh tennis club, she might as well look the part.

\* \* \*

The Rainier tennis club was a bastion of the city's most affluent families, a low sprawling structure situated on the west bank of Lake Washington. At one end of the championship quality courts, there was a wide terrace for spectators, and she found Phil out there, sitting under a striped umbrella, sipping a glass of tomato juice and watching the two men playing tennis in the near court. When he saw Shelley, he raised a hand to beckon her over.

'Is that Jim playing?' she asked, sitting down across the table from him.

'Yes, and as good as he is it looks as though he's met his match.' He nodded in the direction of the court, and, squinting a little against the bright sunlight, Shelley drew in her breath sharply when she recognised his opponent. There was no mistaking the tall form, the black hair.

'I see,' she said. 'It's Blake Fowler, isn't it?'

Phil only nodded, his eyes glued to the two men, who were both playing with set concentration, obviously putting everything they had into the match, slamming the ball back and forth across the net as though it were a hated enemy.

Shelley watched, entranced. It was close all the way, and both seemed bent on victory. Jim was probably the better player, but the younger man had it all over him in sheer muscle power and animal vitality. In fact, seeing Blake like this, his face glistening with perspiration, his dark hair tousled and falling over his forehead, it was as though she was really seeing him for the first time.

His body was all hard, taut muscle, the long legs beneath the brief white shorts, the power in his arms as he raised them up to deliver his strong serves, the agility with which he swooped down to return a ball backhand. Across the net, Jim was having a real run for his money.

It was a very close match, neither man giving any quarter, but in the end, after delivering a spinning ball that simply whizzed past Jim, Blake ended the victor. Smiling, the two men shook hands, and as they came walking slowly towards the terrace Blake pulled his white knit shirt off to wipe his streaming face with it, revealing a smooth well-muscled chest, board-flat abdomen, broad shoulders and a remarkable tan, by Seattle standards.

'Ah, Shelley,' Jim said, as they approached the table. 'Glad to see you got here all right. You were just in time to witness my defeat.' He turned to Blake, who had tossed the white shirt loosely around his shoulders. 'But I claim a rematch.'

Blake nodded, grinning. 'Any time you say.' Then he glanced at Shelley. 'How are you, Shelley?' he asked quietly.

'Fine,' she replied, flashing him a bright smile.

'Well,' Jim said, 'I'm heading for the showers, then I'd like a long cold drink. Will you join us, Blake?'

'No—no, thanks. I'm meeting someone in a little while.'

'Some other time, then.' Jim turned to Phil. 'Phil, if you'll come with me, we can discuss that problem you mentioned.'

Phil jumped to his feet and followed Jim towards the main building, leaving Shelley alone with Blake, and feeling distinctly uneasy about the fact. If he had a date, surely he wouldn't stay, but in the next moment he'd taken the seat Phil had vacated.

'I could use a drink of water,' he said, reaching for a full glass. 'May I?'

'Be my guest,' she replied, and watched as he downed the entire glass in one long gulp.

Sitting so close to all that tanned, muscular naked flesh was making her jumpier by the moment, and somehow watching the long column of his throat as he swallowed, his head thrown back, only increased her nervousness.

'Ah,' he said, setting the glass down, 'that tasted good.' He put his elbows on the table and smiled at her. 'Well, Shelley, how have you been?'

'Oh, fine. Fine. And you?'

'Not bad.'

'It's a beautiful day, isn't it?' she said in a bright tone. 'Unusual for it to be so warm this time of year.'

'Yes, isn't it?'

When the subject of the weather was exhausted, Shelley searched around in her mind for another neutral subject, but nothing even remotely appropriate came to her. *He* didn't seem to be bothered by the awkward situation, just sat there sprawled in his chair, gazing around as though he owned the place. She *wished* Jim would come back.

Finally, just as she was about to make an excuse—anything just to get out of there—he leaned across the table and put his head closer to hers. 'Shelley,' he said in a low voice, 'I've been thinking about calling you, but I wasn't sure what kind of reception I'd get. How about it? I'm a patient man, but if you're still hung up on...'

Then, suddenly, his eyes moved past her, he raised a hand, smiling, and started to rise to his feet. 'I have to go now. My lunch date just showed up, and I still have to shower.'

Unable to stop herself, Shelley turned around to see one of the more glamorous local television newswomen standing near the entrance waving at Blake. 'Well,' she said tartly, looking up at him, 'I see you didn't waste any time finding a new playmate.'

His eyes narrowed down at her. 'Since you weren't interested, you hardly have cause for complaint,' he snapped.

She knew instantly that she'd sounded just like a jealous woman, and could have bitten her tongue out the moment the words were out of her mouth. 'I'm sorry,' she said. 'I shouldn't have said that.'

'No, you shouldn't,' he replied in a curt tone, and with that he turned abruptly and stalked off.

Just at that moment Phil and Jim returned. After ordering drinks, they got right down to their business meeting, but Shelley could hardly keep her mind on the discussion. All she could think about was that stupid remark she'd made to Blake and wonder what in the world had possessed her to say such a thing.

From then on, with all the last-minute demands of the campaign to attend to, the days flew by. It was the middle of October, only a few weeks away from the election, and according to the polls Jim was so far ahead of his opponent that victory was virtually a certainty.

Shelley hadn't seen or heard from Blake at all since the day at the tennis club. He hadn't tried to contact her at all, and in an odd way she missed him. She found herself thinking about him often, wondering if she hadn't been too hasty in dismissing him so finally, and still regretting what she'd said to him at their last encounter.

Then she would remember how much he resembled David—the same feckless charm, the same irresponsible attitude towards women, seeing them as objects to be lured into bed rather than as human beings, and would congratulate herself on her narrow escape from repeating the same mistake all over again.

That Saturday night there was to be a gala formal affair at the Four Seasons hotel to wind things up, a gesture of thanks Jim wanted to make to all his supporters. For Shelley it was virtually a command performance, and although she was exhausted by her recent efforts on Jim's behalf she was looking forward to it. The end of the campaign meant that Jim's obligation to the Talbots was also over, and for his sake she wanted to look her very best tonight.

She hadn't had a spare moment to shop for a new outfit, but it had been so long since she'd worn any of her old dresses that they might as well be new. In the end, she chose one of her favourites, a slim green silk sheath that just matched the colour of her eyes. The bodice was strapless, and cut quite low, but with an overlay of sheer georgette that toned down its suggestive qualities.

Phil had offered to pick her up, but she'd declined. If she took a cab, there was always the hope that Jim would drive her home.

That hope blossomed when she arrived at the ballroom of the hotel. She stood in the entrance for a few moments scanning the crowd, and finally spotted Jim off in a corner talking to a group of people, among whom were the elder Talbots. But Vanessa was not among them.

Shelley's heart soared. Ordinarily the blonde stuck like glue to Jim's side during these events. Of course, she could be in the powder-room, or simply late, but Shelley wasn't going to pass up the opportunity for some time alone with him, even if it was only for a few minutes.

She had just started across the crowded dance-floor towards him when she felt a hand on her arm, and she turned to see Phil at her side. Grinning broadly, he moved in front of her, took her hands in his, then stood back, his eyes sweeping over her with open approval.

'My,' he exclaimed, 'don't you look gorgeous to-night!' He tucked her arm under his. 'In fact,' he went on in a quieter, more intimate voice, 'if I didn't know your heart lay elsewhere, I'd try my luck with you myself.'

She flicked him a sideways glance. 'Sure you would,' she commented wryly. Then she smiled. 'You're so wedded to your work you don't have time for romance, and you know it.'

'Well, you're in luck tonight anyway,' he said, heading towards Jim. 'The blonde limpet isn't here. Now's your big chance.'

Shelley frowned and tugged her arm free. 'It's not exactly a contest, Phil,' she said in a dry tone. 'Jim's a free agent.'

They had arrived at Jim's group by now. He was in the centre of it, his expression serious, listening intently to Mr Talbot expounding on his pet peeves.

Shelley held back, standing beside Mrs Talbot and watching. Jim was smiling now, and as he raised his eyes to include the rest of the circle they fell on Shelley. The smile widened and he nodded at her, but it wasn't until the music started and the others began to drift on to the dance-floor that he moved to her side.

'Shelley,' he said in a low voice, 'you look very beautiful tonight.' His eyes swept over the green dress. 'My favourite colour too.' Then he spread his arms wide. 'Will you dance with me?'

With a glad smile, she moved happily into his arms, and they danced out into the middle of the floor. He held her loosely, and neither of them spoke for some time. There was no need for words. It had been months since she'd been this close to him, and she wanted to enjoy every moment of it.

'Well, Shelley,' he said at last, smiling down at her, 'in just a few weeks it will all be over.'

'Yes,' she replied. 'And you'll be our new governor.'

'It really does look that way, doesn't it?' he said musingly. He shook his head. 'It's still hard to believe. You know I couldn't have done it without you.'

Shelley stiffened a little in his arms. Was he referring to the episode with Blake Fowler again? But she'd explained that to him already, and thought she'd convinced him nothing had happened. Well, almost nothing. Surely Jim didn't still believe she'd seduced the man just to get him elected?

She gave him a troubled look. 'Jim,' she said slowly, 'if you're talking about Blake Fowler, let me tell you again that I didn't do anything to change his mind.'

His arms tightened around her. 'Of course not. I only meant all your hard work, the long hours you've put in on the campaign, your loyalty and commitment. There's no way I can ever thank you enough for all that.'

'You don't have to,' she assured him hurriedly. 'I did it all because I believed in you.' And loved you, she added silently. But she couldn't tell him that. It was up to him now. He had to know how she felt about him. Even Phil knew that!

He pressed his cheek against hers and gave a low chuckle into her ear. 'You'll have to admit, though, that the real turning point came when Fowler's newspaper came out on my side. And no matter what you say I'm convinced you had something to do with it.'

Shelley sighed. If he wanted to believe that, there was no way she could talk him out of it. And perhaps he was right. She recalled the conversation she'd had with Blake about his duty to the public to choose sides in such an important election. Maybe that had had some effect. Just so long as Jim didn't think . . .

But her thoughts broke off as she found herself gazing directly into a familiar pair of startling blue eyes. He was sitting with five or six other people at one of the round tables placed around the dance-floor. For the space of a heartbeat, that limpid blue gaze held her prisoner, but the minute she came to her senses she quickly looked away.

When she dared to glance back at the table again she saw that he'd turned around and was speaking to the attractive dark-haired woman sitting beside him—the same one, she realised with a slight shock of recognition, who had been with him the first night they'd met, in this very hotel, as a matter of fact.

Suddenly, for some crazy reason, Shelley became filled with a rush of resentment. Wouldn't you know? The man was insatiable. Couldn't he go for five minutes without some adoring female hanging on to him? She went on silently in that vein for some time, until finally a terrible thought came to her.

Once again she was sounding very much like a jealous woman! But that couldn't be. Here she was, in the arms of the man she loved at last, free of the hateful Vanessa, a rosy future before her, a real chance that she might end up the wife of the governor in time. What did she care what Blake Fowler did, or who he did it with?

She was so wrapped up in her thoughts that she didn't realise Jim had danced her straight towards Blake's table until he stopped just behind his chair. Startled, she looked down to see that Jim was tapping Blake on the shoulder to get his attention.

When he turned around, he looked up at Jim with a level gaze, then flicked his eyes briefly at Shelley. He nodded shortly at her, then rose to his feet and held out his hand to Jim.

'Good evening, Governor,' he said, a wry, slightly mocking smile playing about his lips.

Jim laughed and grasped Blake's hand, shaking it warmly. 'A little premature, aren't you?'

Blake shrugged. 'I don't think there's any doubt about the outcome now.'

'Thanks to you, Blake,' Jim said. He gave the hand one last warm shake, then dropped it. 'You were the catalyst that put me over the top, and I'm very grateful.'

'Don't thank me. I was only doing my duty.' The blue eyes flashed briefly at Shelley, then back at Jim. 'All the thanks I want is that you be a good governor.'

'Oh, you can count on that!' Jim replied. He took Shelley by the arm. 'Of course, you already know Shelley. My indispensable right hand.'

'Of course,' Blake murmured. Then he glanced down at the brunette and put his hand on her shoulder. She had been gazing up at the little scene with an enquiring expression on her lovely face, and was now rising slowly to her feet. As Shelley got her first close look at her, she realised that the woman was much older than she'd appeared at a distance, and that fact gave her a perverse sense of satisfaction.

'Annette,' Blake was saying to her now, 'may I present our next governor, Jim Carruthers? And his assistant, Miss Dalton. Jim, I'd like you to meet my sister.'

'A great pleasure, Miss Fowler,' Jim said, holding out a hand and warmly grasping hers.

The brunette laughed. 'It's Mrs Conrad, actually. I'm an old married woman.'

His sister! Shelley could only stand there stunned. Of course! On closer examination the resemblance was unmistakable. The same almost-black hair and startling blue eyes, even the same rather mocking smile. She was even more astounded, however, at the waves of relief that washed over her.

The next thing she knew Jim had asked Annette Conrad to dance with him, and Shelley was left standing there facing Blake. She sneaked a quick glance at him to see if he'd sensed her discomposure and was laughing at her, but instead the expression on his lean face was remote, even grave.

'Would you care to dance?' he asked easily.

It was on the tip of her tongue to refuse, but in the next moment she changed her mind. Why not? It certainly couldn't hurt Jim to keep a powerful newspaper like the *News-Tribune* on his side. There was no point in offending him.

'Yes,' she replied, nodding, 'I would.'

It seemed quite natural to be in his arms again as he led her deftly out into the middle of the crowded floor. He held her loosely, even sedately, humming a little under his breath along with the orchestra, as was his habit, and as they danced along in silence she found herself automatically comparing him with Jim once again.

The difference was that Jim made her feel safe, that was it, while in spite of Blake's cool air of unconcern there was an explosive quality about him, of pent-up energy that could erupt at any moment, even a potential for violence she felt she had to protect herself against.

But against what? Well, he had come on rather strong in the beginning. Apparently, however, he'd given up, and, while that was definitely what she wanted, at the same time she felt oddly let down. It was almost as though a light had been dimmed in her life.

Or, more accurately, she thought wryly as he pulled her tightly up against his long, lean body to avoid a collision with another couple, as though a dangerous wild animal, a tiger perhaps, had decided not to have her for dinner after all.

Just then the sound of his voice broke into her wayward thoughts. 'Well, Shelley, how have you been?'

She jumped a little and looked up to see him smiling down at her, his expression bland, not in the least threatening, and she had to smile at the fanciful picture of him she had just built up in her mind. There was no danger here.

'Quite well,' she replied. 'Busy, of course, with all the last-minute details to take care of before the election.'

'Well, it'll soon be over, then you can take a nice long rest.' He paused for a moment. 'What are you plans?'

'Well, the first thing on my agenda is a trip home to visit my parents. It's been months since I've seen them. They weren't young when I was born, and are getting on in years now.'

'But they're all right?' he asked, with what seemed to be genuine concern. 'I mean, there's no emergency is there?'

'I'm not sure,' she said slowly. 'I talked to my mother a while ago, and it seems my father suffered a mild heart attack last month. She assured me it was nothing serious, that he'd just have to start taking it a little easier. And she must be telling me the truth, since they didn't even let me know about it when it happened.'

'Still, you're worried about it?' he asked softly.

'Well, yes, I am. Most of all, though, I guess I feel a little guilty about the way I've been neglecting them. As the only child of rather elderly parents, I feel an obligation to them, and I'm afraid I've let them down.'

'What's the prognosis, then, about your father's condition?'

'All Mother said was that he was supposed to be resting more.' She laughed. 'Dad may be getting on in years, but you'd never know it from the way he slaves at that silly little newspaper of his. It's the great love of his life.'

'Then he's a lucky man, isn't he? I mean, to have something he cares about that much.'

'Yes, I suppose so,' she said slowly. 'But I still worry.'

'Well, as I said, it'll soon be over.'

Just then Jim danced by with Annette Conrad, deep in conversation, and Shelley looked up at Blake. 'Your sister is a very attractive woman,' she said. 'In fact,' she added without thinking, 'she's very much like you.'

Blake threw back his head and laughed explosively. 'Does that mean you think I'm attractive too?' he finally asked, his mouth still twitching with amusement. 'If so,' he went on in a dry tone, 'you have a most peculiar way of showing it.'

Flustered, she groped around for a safer subject. 'Is Annette up here on a visit?'

He nodded. 'She lives in San Francisco and has five children; she needs to escape from time to time. Although my brother-in-law is a fairly affluent doctor, Annette's one of those old-fashioned women who believe a mother should raise her own children. But she does need an occasional holiday. Which,' he added, 'I'm most happy to provide. Like you, I don't see my family nearly as often as I'd like.'

The orchestra stopped playing just then, and Blake released her. There was a light smattering of applause, and she was about to turn away, but before she could take a step the music started up again, a slow tune, and Blake reached out for her again.

'I think I've had enough for now,' she said, stepping back from him. 'I've hardly mingled at all since I got here, and I expect Jim will be looking for me.'

'Ah, yes,' he said, stepping back and giving her a long look. 'Jim.' He took her by the arm and led her off the dance-floor towards the back of the room, where it was quieter. 'I suppose that will all be decided now. Have you made any definite plans?'

'No,' she said in some confusion. 'Not yet.'

'But you still have hope.'

'I'd really rather not discuss it,' she said stiffly. She shrugged. 'There's nothing actually to discuss.'

'You do still want him, though,' he persisted.

She didn't know how to answer him. There really wasn't much point in evading the issue. He knew quite well how she felt about Jim. She wasn't ashamed of it. Still, until the election was safely over she didn't dare reveal her true feelings openly to anyone.

At the door to the powder-room, she turned to him. 'I'll leave you now,' she said. 'It was nice to see you again.'

Blake gave her a quizzical look, then released her arm. 'Good luck in the election.'

'Thank you,' she said, and with a quick smile pushed the door open and stepped through it.

Inside the powder-room, she breathed a sigh of relief as the door swung to, blocking him from sight, then glanced around. There were three other occupants, all of them standing before the long mirror above the washbasins repairing their make-up or fiddling with their hair.

And one of them, she saw as she came closer, was Vanessa Talbot! So she'd shown up after all! Shelley fought down her dismay, put on her brightest smile, and walked over to her.

'Hello, Vanessa,' she said. 'Glad you were able to make it.'

The blonde turned slowly and gave Shelley a cool look. 'Are you really?' she drawled. She turned back to the mirror. 'Of course I came. This is a big night for Jim, and I knew he'd want me to share it with him.'

Shelley gritted her teeth, biting back the sharp retort, then set her bag down on the shelf and took out her comb. As she ran it through her hair, she glanced over at the blonde's reflection. It was the first time she'd had a close look at her under bright lights, and what she saw reassured her.

For all Vanessa's expensive clothes, her carefully styled hair, her perfect make-up, her flashing diamonds, she actually wasn't a beautiful woman, hardly even a pretty one. Her eyes were too small, her hairline too low, her mouth definitely mean and pouting.

Although the professional make-up job did a lot to disguise these defects, Shelley felt a warm rush of relief at the sight of what lay beneath the hard veneer. Jim could never love a woman like that, and poor Vanessa would find that out eventually. Shelley could even pity her a little. Certainly she could afford to be generous, to allow the blonde her moment of triumph tonight. After the election, it would all be over for her.

When the other women were gone, Shelley collected her things and started towards the door. Before she reached it, however, it opened and Annette Conrad walked inside. When she noticed Shelley, her eyes lit up, eyes that could have been Blake's.

'Well, hello again,' she said, smiling broadly. 'How nice to see you again, Shelley.' She walked past her towards the mirror, set down her handbag, then turned around. 'Blake has told me so much about you,' she added warmly.

'Oh, really?' Shelley was amazed that Blake had discussed her at all with his sister. 'You too,' she added hurriedly. 'I mean, he mentioned that you lived in San Francisco, that your husband was a doctor, and that you had five children.'

Annette laughed. 'That sounds like my brother, boring everybody with my life history. Believe me, it's even duller than he tells it.' She took a brush out of her bag and ran it over her short dark hair. 'But it suits me. Now your work sounds exciting. Blake tells me that you've been instrumental in what looks like a certain victory for Mr Carruthers. You must be very proud.'

Shelley smiled, warming to the friendly brunette. 'Well, I wouldn't exactly say instrumental, but I've done my best.'

'Obviously it's paid off.' Annette hesitated, then went on in a more halting tone, 'I hope I'm not treading on forbidden territory, but Blake did mention that there was a more personal element to your relationship with Mr Carruthers.'

Shelley shrugged. 'We're good friends,' she said in what she hoped was a non-committal tone.

'Oh, of course,' Annette said quickly. 'I understand. Sorry if I overstepped.' She laughed. 'It's a family trait, I'm afraid, to barge in where we have no business.' She snapped her handbag shut and came over to Shelley. 'I guess I was hoping my feckless brother had decided to settle down at last. From the way he talked about you——' She broke off with a shrug. 'But that's not my business either, is it? Are you going back? I'll walk along with you, if you don't mind. I hear the orchestra has quit playing, so I imagine the programme is about to begin.'

Shelley spent the rest of the evening listening to a lot of boring speeches, chewing her way through a tasteless dinner, and watching Vanessa pawing Jim. Nor did she miss the smug looks directed her way by the blonde, whose arrival, of course, put paid to Shelley's hopes for any more personal conversation with Jim, much less a ride home.

She excused herself early, before the second round of dancing started, and slipped away quietly. Her facial muscles were aching from smiling, her back teeth sore from being clamped together.

It was only a short cab ride, and when she got home she undressed hurriedly and fell into bed. But sleep wouldn't come immediately, as she'd hoped, and as she tossed and turned the brief conversation she'd had with Blake's sister kept popping into her head. What had she meant when she'd said she'd hoped her brother had decided to 'settle down at last'?

Fat chance of that! And just how had he spoken of her to Annette, to make her think she would have anything to do with the possibility, however hopeless? But it was pointless to speculate about that, and, banishing all thoughts of Blake Fowler from her mind, Shelley shifted her position once again. Just a few short weeks, she kept reminding herself. Then it would all be over.

But, in spite of her good intentions, the last image in her mind as she drifted off to sleep was of a tall dark man with flashing blue eyes and a mocking smile.

It rained on election day, which meant a light turn-out. Phil assured Shelley that this was all to the good, since it would be the fence-straddlers who would stay home, but Shelley wasn't convinced, and remained on pins and needles all day until eight o'clock, when the polls closed.

They were all gathered together at Jim's head-quarters when the first returns started to trickle in. Shelley had been there since early morning herself, telephoning prospective voters with last-minute pleas for their support, offering transportation. Gradually others began to appear, and by now the large room was quite crowded.

There was a jubilant feeling in the air, even before there were any real indications of how the election had gone, and by nine Jim was apparently so far ahead his opponent would never catch up. Several reporters had already straggled in, and the crowd was waiting expectantly for Jim himself to show up to make his victory speech.

At midnight, the other candidate appeared on television to concede his defeat. A loud cheer went up, which escalated into a deafening roar when Jim himself came through the door, beaming, his arms raised above his head, his hands clasped in a symbol of victory.

'Speech! Speech!' shouted the crowd as he made his way to the small platform at the far end of the room.

Watching him from a distance, so triumphant in his victory, looking every inch a statesman-like leader, Shelley felt her heart almost burst with pride, not only because she'd played such a key role in his success, but even more because now a personal future with him would be possible.

As he grasped the microphone and raised a hand, the noise of the crowd abated gradually, until finally there was complete silence in the room. First he warmly thanked all his supporters, mentioning Phil Dorsey and Shelley herself as foremost among them, then went on to outline what he hoped to accomplish during the next four years.

When he finished, there was deafening applause and another great roar of approval. Apparently he wasn't finished, however, and after a few minutes he raised his hand again for silence. When it had quietened down, he began speaking again, this time in a more serious tone.

'I'd like to end on a more personal note,' he said. 'You all know how much I owe to the Talbot family for their faith in me, their unstinting support, both financial and moral.' He paused for a moment. 'And now,' he went on, 'just this evening, they presented me with yet another gift.' Smiling, he reached out a hand to the front row. 'Their lovely daughter, Vanessa, has done me the honour of accepting my proposal of marriage.'

Shelley stared as a beaming Vanessa took hold of Jim's outstretched hand and joined him on the platform. At first she was too stunned to take it all in. Had she heard him right? But there was Vanessa, standing beside him now, beaming up at him, a look of triumph on her face. Jim's arm was around her, and he leaned over to kiss her on the cheek as the photographers' flash bulbs popped.

The room began to spin before Shelley's eyes, and her stomach lurched sickeningly as waves of nausea swept over her. She was having trouble breathing. Air! she thought. I need some air!

She turned and stumbled blindly towards the exit, bumping into people as she went, until she finally reached the door to the small entrance hall, the noise of the crowd still drumming in her ears. In a daze, she walked unsteadily over to the coat rack along the wall to retrieve her jacket. She was just struggling into it, fumbling with the buttons, when through the turmoil raging within her she suddenly became aware that someone was standing just beyond the doorway to the main room.

She looked up, and was horrified to see that it was Blake. For a moment their eyes locked together, and she couldn't move. The familiar faintly mocking smile curled on his lips, which was bad enough, but as she met the bright blue gaze she saw only pity there, and she didn't know which was worse.

He raised a hand towards her, then let it drop helplessly at his side, but made no move towards her. With a strangled sob, she whirled around and stumbled out through the main door.

Outside on the pavement the snow was sprinkling lightly. Shelley started to run, her one thought to get away, as far as possible from the hateful scene. As she ran, she thought she heard someone call her name, but by now she had reached her car. She got inside and drove off, hardly seeing where she was going.

# CHAPTER SIX

THREE weeks later Shelley was in the big old-fashioned kitchen of her parents' house helping her mother prepare Thanksgiving dinner. There had been a light snowfall the night before, and as she gazed out of the window at the white blanket, dazzling under a pale sun, she felt a deep sense of peace.

'Mother,' she said, 'you must be expecting an army for dinner today, with all this food. Who's coming, anyway?'

'Oh, just the usual,' her mother replied vaguely.

Shelley smiled. Her mother was famous in their small community not only for taking in every stray animal that came along, but for including all the friends she knew would be alone on such an important holiday in their own family celebration.

With a sigh, Shelley set the cranberries on the stove to boil. 'So we're talking about twenty people, I take it.'

'More or less. I think your father may have asked a few business associates.'

Shelley rolled her eyes. Better make it twenty-five, and she added another handful of berries, more water and sugar.

Ever since her hurried retreat from Jim's victory celebration and her equally swift trip north the very next day she'd been constantly amazed at how quickly she'd recovered from what had seemed at the time a fatal blow. It had taken only a few days and one long tearful conversation with her mother to convince her that her heart wasn't broken after all, that actually only her pride was hurt.

In fact, she could hardly believe now that she'd ever imagined she was in love with Jim Carruthers, even before he'd betrayed her trust in him so callously. She was still angry with him for leading her on the way he had just so long as she was useful to him, then cutting her out of his life without any explanation or preparation, but all she felt about him personally now was that she'd had a very narrow escape.

She realised too that what suffering she had gone through for his sake those first few days after he had announced his engagement to Vanessa Talbot in front of the whole world had been far more the result of shock than unrequited love. Loving Jim had been a habit, not at all the deep emotion she had thought.

The one recurring image that still had the power to disturb her was that last glimpse of Blake Fowler, the knowing little smile, the pity in his eyes. And the way he'd deceived her about supporting Jim still rankled. He was just like all the rest, David, Phil and Jim included. At least she hadn't been fool enough to fall for him, and she clung to that one remnant of pride she had left with all her might.

It helped too, that she'd been so busy since coming home. Although her father's illness didn't seem to be life-threatening, it was true that he had to slow down, and Shelley had taken it upon herself immediately to do what she could to help him on the newspaper. Luckily she'd saved quite a bit of money from the excellent salary Jim had paid her, so she didn't need to ask her parents for help.

Although she was still learning the ropes, a lot had come back to her from the days when she used to help out after school, on weekends and summer holidays. She was finding that not only was the work absorbing, but she seemed to be good at it, and was doubly gratified that she really seemed to be helping her father.

The cranberries had started to boil by now. She turned down the burner, then poured herself a fresh cup of coffee and went over to the worktable in the middle of the room to watch her mother stuffing the enormous turkey.

'Mother,' she said, 'do you think Dad will decide to sell the newspaper after all?'

Her mother gave her a sharp look. 'I don't know. The doctor and I tried to talk him into it at first, and of course he resisted. You know how he loves that paper. He's always said he was born with printer's ink in his veins.' She gave Shelley a warm smile. 'But since you've been here it's taken a lot of the burden off his shoulders.'

'But do you think I've helped him enough?'

'Oh, yes.' Her mother went over to the sink to wash her hands. 'But then you may not want to stay. And you shouldn't stay just for his sake,' she added hastily. 'He's had two or three excellent offers to buy the paper, so you needn't think we'll starve if he does give it up.'

Shelley drained her coffee, set the cup down on the table, then leaned her hips back against it, her arms folded in front of her. 'Well, I've been thinking I might want to stay on anyway. I mean, for my own sake, not necessarily just to help Dad out.'

'Really?' her mother asked in pleased surprise. She laughed. 'Somehow I hadn't expected you'd want to bury yourself up here after the fast pace and excitement of city life.'

'Oh, I've had quite enough of that!' Shelley replied firmly.

Her mother gave her a long careful look, her lips pursed thoughtfully. 'And what about your interest in politics?'

Shelley threw up her hands. 'Believe me, I've had all I want of politics to last me the rest of my life!' She shook her head sadly. 'I was a fool to get involved in it in the first place.'

'Oh, I don't think so,' her mother said calmly as she laced up the turkey. 'It was a good experience for you, something you had to do.' She smiled at Shelley, her eyes twinkling. 'And it doesn't seem to me you've suffered any permanent damage from it.'

'No, I haven't, but I still feel like every kind of fool for letting that man walk all over me. You'd think after my experience with David I'd have known better.'

'Oh, one of these days the right man will come along for you, darling—I feel sure of it. Everyone's entitled to a few mistakes—that's how we learn. And as I say, no real harm has been done. You're still young, a very lovely girl, even if I do say so myself, and you have a lot to offer a man.'

Shelley laughed. 'Not that you're prejudiced,' she said teasingly.

Her mother sniffed. 'Not at all.' She picked up the roasting-pan and went over to the oven. 'Now, I'd better get this bird in or it won't be ready in time.'

As Shelley watched her, still glowing from her praise, an image of Blake Fowler suddenly popped into her head, not for the first time since she'd been home. It was funny how Jim had slipped from her mind so completely, but the memory of the time she'd spent with Blake lingered on.

Nor could she get that one brief conversation she'd had with his sister out of her mind, couldn't help wondering what she'd meant by it, or what would have happened between them if it hadn't been for her stupid obsession with Jim.

She gave herself a little shake and went over to take the cranberries off the stove. There was no point in dwelling on what might have been. And, considering the kind of man Blake obviously was, there surely had never been a chance of a future with him anyway.

The dinner guests were due to arrive at five o'clock. At four-thirty Shelley had finished dressing, and it was time to go downstairs to help her mother take care of any last-minute details.

A new bank of heavy black clouds had drifted in that afternoon, threatening another even heavier snowfall, and it was already beginning to grow dark outside. But the house was cosy and warm, and in a small town there weren't such great distances for people to travel, so she expected the full contingent of guests would show up.

In fact, she could already hear voices drifting up from downstairs. Since the doorbell hadn't rung, it must be her father. He'd spent the day at the office, as usual, even on a holiday. As she gave herself one last quick once-over in the mirror, even she could see the change in her appearance from the pale, rather pathetic creature who'd shown up on her parents' doorstep three weeks ago.

The deep rust-coloured woollen dress she'd chosen was just the colour of her hair, which now shone with new highlights that had been dimmed before, and her skin had taken on a healthy glow from being out of doors so much in the brisk country air.

She switched off her bedroom light and started downstairs. The voices seemed to be coming from the living-room now, where she'd laid a fire earlier. Her mother must have lit it while she was getting ready, since she could already smell the woodsmoke. At the bottom of the stairs she turned into the wide archway that led from the entrance hall to the living-room, a smile of greeting already formed on her lips.

But the smile became frozen in place when her eye fell on the small group standing in front of the fire—her mother and two men. One was her father, and the other, of all people, was Blake Fowler, in the flesh, the last person she had ever expected to see again, much less in her own home.

For a moment she felt so disorientated that all she could do was stand there staring stupidly at him. Although he was turned slightly away from her, there was enough of his profile showing to see quite clearly who he was. Besides, she would recognise that tall figure and dark head anywhere.

Her immediate thought was how glad she was that even in their most confidential talks she'd never even mentioned Blake's name to her mother. But what in the world was he doing here? Surely if he'd come to seek her out he would have contacted her directly.

Just then her father looked up and caught her eye. 'Ah, here she is now. Come in, Shelley. There's someone here I want you to meet.'

Blake turned slowly around to face her, blue eyes glinting in the glow of the fire, the familiar slightly mocking smile on his lips. Pulling herself together, Shelley gave him a cool smile, then dropped her eyes and started walking towards her father. Not for worlds did she want either of her parents to know they were already acquainted. He was part of a past she only wanted to forget.

'Shelley,' her father said, putting an arm around her, 'this is Blake Fowler.' He laughed. 'A city slicker up from Seattle who wants to buy my paper. Blake, my daughter Shelley.'

'How do you do?' Shelley murmured, giving him a quick warning glance.

'Shelley,' he said, turning an impassive gaze on her. Then his lips began to twitch ominously, and for a moment she was terrified he was going to let the cat out of the bag. Instead, he gave her a slight bow and held out a hand. There was no way she could avoid taking it, but when she tried to withdraw it he held on to it a few moments longer, pressing it tightly in his own, as though sending her a private message, even reassuring her that he'd got the message and was willing to play along with her.

'How about a glass of sherry?' her father said, going over to the sideboard and taking down the wine glasses. 'Blake? Or would you rather have something stronger?'

'Sherry will be fine,' Blake replied.

Just then the doorbell rang, and Shelley's mother turned to her husband. 'No wine for me, John,' she said. 'Our guests have started to arrive.'

'I'll get the door, Mother,' Shelley said quickly. 'You sit down and relax.'

'Oh, no, dear, you stay and entertain Mr Fowler. Come on, John, it's time to play host.'

He opened his mouth to protest, but clamped it shut when he saw the determined look on her face. With a swift glance at Shelley, he shrugged and turned to follow his wife out of the room, grumbling a little under his breath.

When her parents were gone, Shelley went swiftly to Blake's side and glared up at him. 'What are you doing here?' she whispered fiercely.

He set his glass down carefully on the mat and gave her a look of innocent surprise. 'Why, your father invited me, of course.' He grinned. 'Quite a friendly man, your father.'

'You mean gullible, don't you? Well, don't be too sure. He's not as naïve as he looks, and if you have any diabolical scheme in your head of stealing his newspaper——'

'Hey!' he broke in. 'Hold on. Aren't you getting a little carried away?' He picked up his glass and took a slow sip of wine, gazing steadily at her over the rim. 'Now, I gathered from the icy look you gave me when you first saw me that you didn't want them to know we'd already met, and I very graciously went along with you. But naturally I'm curious. Why all the secrecy?'

She eyed him balefully, every nerve twanging, still reeling from the shock of seeing him here at all. *He* seemed perfectly at ease, just standing there drinking his sherry, his eyes fastened on her in a look of tolerant indulgence, waiting for an answer to his question.

Actually, she couldn't think of one, except that she felt instinctively that his presence meant danger to her personally, let alone her father's business, and she could hardly tell him that.

'Come on, Shelley,' he prodded, 'you must have a reason. Are you ashamed of me? Actually, I'm quite well house-trained. I won't disgrace you by getting drunk or eating with my fingers or telling off-colour stories.'

From the entrance hall came the sound of loud voices as the elder Daltons welcomed the new arrivals. Soon they would be coming inside the living-room to join them. There was no hope of getting rid of Blake now, unless she could convince him to leave of his own accord, manufacture a pressing engagement or sudden illness.

'I just don't want you here, that's all,' she finally blurted out. 'Isn't that enough?'

Blake gave her a broad smile. 'Afraid not.'

Just then the others came bursting inside. Most of them were old friends of Shelley's parents whom she'd known since childhood, and she was immediately swept up in a round of warm greetings. Apparently Blake was determined to stand his ground, and she couldn't very well order him out of the house. She would just have to make the best of a very sticky situation and hope he took his leave early.

Actually, the dinner went off more smoothly than Shelley had feared. Blake was a perfect guest, and ended by charming the socks off every female present, her mother included. He was an entertaining talker, with a fund of amusing stories about his newspaper experiences, yet able to listen so intently when someone else had the floor, no matter how boring they were with their small-town gossip, that he had to be either a consummate actor or genuinely interested.

Still, she was on guard all through the meal, watching him and listening to him carefully, ready to steer the conversation away if it turned to any topic that touched on their mutual past.

She'd recovered her composure to a large extent by now, and, while his model behaviour throughout dinner gradually allayed her fears, she was still determined to get him out of the house—out of the *town*, for that matter—as quickly as possible. By now she was convinced that he'd shown up out of the blue like this for one of two reasons—either to gloat over the humiliation she'd suffered at Jim Carruthers' hands, or to offer her sympathy, a shoulder to cry on.

Either one was simply intolerable to her. That experience still had the power to fill her with anger and shame, not because of losing Jim to Vanessa, but because she'd made such a fool of herself. Blake had witnessed that humiliation. His very presence in the house was a bitter reminder of an episode in her life she only wanted to forget, *had* forgotten until he'd appeared.

To her intense relief, almost immediately after the stuffed diners had finished their pumpkin pie and coffee and her mother had risen from her chair to clear the table, he stood up to take his leave. He very graciously thanked her mother for the dinner, and flatly refused her father's offer of a ride back to the local inn, where he was staying.

'No, thanks, John,' he said quite firmly. 'It's not that far, and I need to walk off some of your wife's marvellous cooking.'

'But it's snowing!' her mother protested. 'And it's a good eight blocks' walk. You'll be soaked!'

'Shelley,' her father broke in, 'why don't you drive Blake to the inn?'

Shelley opened her mouth to protest, but stopped herself. If she didn't do it, she knew her father would, and she didn't want him to take any risks with his precarious state of health. Not only that, but it would give her a chance to be alone with Blake so that she could get the issue of his presence in town settled.

'Sure, Dad,' she said, rising from her chair, 'I'd be glad to.' She glanced at Blake. 'I'll just get my things.'

Although the snowfall was rather heavy, with large soft flakes coming down in a steady stream, it was also slushy, the temperature still warm enough so that it hadn't yet iced over, and the driving conditions weren't dangerous.

The minute they were inside the car and Shelley had started the engine, she turned to Blake and gave him a challenging look. 'Now,' she said in a determined voice, 'I want the truth. Why have you really come here?'

'Suspicious little thing, aren't you?' he commented with a smile of amusement.

'Blake,' she said in a warning tone, 'I've just about had it with your jokes at my expense.'

'All right,' he said, holding up a hand, 'don't bite. I'm sorry. It's just that you're so easy to tease.' He shifted around in his seat so that he was facing her directly. 'Now, seriously, I came for exactly the reason I gave your father. I heard he was thinking about selling his newspaper, and I might be interested in buying it.'

'Why?' she snapped. The motor had warmed enough by now, and she cautiously started backing out of the driveway.

'I'm always on the look-out for good investments,' he went on as she pulled out into the deserted street. 'I can't see why it bothers you so much. I thought you'd be grateful.'

'Hah!' she snorted, shifting gears viciously. 'And the fact that he's my father had nothing to do with it.'

'Don't flatter yourself,' he said in a harder tone. 'You made it perfectly clear you weren't interested in any kind of involvement with me, and, as I told you once, I never beg. Your father wants to sell; I may be in the market to buy. It's that simple.'

She gave him a quick sideways glance. His face was turned in profile now, and he was gazing straight ahead, his eyes narrowed, his jaw set.

Maybe he was telling the truth. Maybe he hadn't come for the reasons she'd first suspected—either to jeer or offer pity.

'Well,' she said at last, 'I apologise if I doubted your intentions, but the fact of the matter is, I don't want my father to sell the paper. I've been working with him for the past few weeks, and find I like it. Actually, I'm going to try to talk him into keeping it and letting me run it. With his advice and counsel, of course.'

The truth was, that intention hadn't really been formed in her mind until that moment. Somehow, the possibility that someone else might buy and run the paper made her realise how much she wanted to keep it in the family. Not only would it provide work for her that she had come to enjoy immensely, but it would allow her father to keep his hand in while she learned, without burdening him with the full responsibility for it.

'I think that's a splendid idea,' Blake said, turning to her.

She gave him a wary glance. 'You do?'

'Absolutely. There's no reason on earth why you and your father shouldn't continue to run the paper. I'm looking into it purely as a business investment. As you know, I don't really care much about editorial policies. Unless,' he added with a grin, 'I'm forced into it by some public-spirited do-gooder who convinces me that it's my duty.'

For a moment she was taken aback by this reference to her attempts to persuade him to support Jim, but the idea that she might actually have had some impact on his decision to do so intrigued her.

She gave him a grudging smile. 'Are you trying to tell me that what I said to you about that made a difference?'

'Of course,' he replied promptly. 'But that was a special case. Ordinarily I keep my hands off editorial policy. And if your father left the business end of running his paper to me, it would take a lot of the burden off him.'

'I don't know,' she said slowly. 'I'll have to think about it. It may not be such a bad idea at that. But of course the final decision is up to my father.'

They had reached the inn by now, a sprawling two-storey structure that had once been a private mansion, the home of one of the town's most affluent families. A local couple had bought it a few years ago and converted it into a pleasant lodge that was close enough to the nearby ski-slopes to attract a steady stream of guests, especially during the winter months.

Shelley turned into the curving drive and stopped the car in front of the wide covered porch that stretched across the front. Although she kept the motor running, Blake made no move to get out.

'I'll tell you what,' he said, reaching for the door-handle. 'Why don't you come inside and have a drink with me and we can discuss the details?'

'Oh, I don't know,' she replied. 'My parents will be expecting me back right away.'

'One drink won't take that long,' he urged.

She thought a moment, then switched off the engine. 'All right,' she agreed reluctantly.

There was still something about the man that made her wary of him, but if he really meant what he said about leaving the running of the paper up to her father it might work out quite well. She herself had no interest in the financial aspect, and with a wealthy backer like Blake a load would be lifted from both their shoulders.

Inside, the lobby was deserted. The heavier snowfalls wouldn't start until December, so it was still a little early for the skiing season. Besides, the Thanksgiving holiday kept most families at home. Shelley turned in the direction of the small bar, but before she'd taken a step Blake grasped her by the arm and was heading for the stairs.

She stopped in her tracks. 'Where are you going?'

He turned to her. 'To my room, of course. Suite, actually.'

She shook her arm free and gave him a disgusted look. 'You never give up, do you?'

He put his hands on his hips and glared down at her. 'The bar happens to be closed,' he snapped. 'I told you I had a suite. That means a sitting-room as well as a bedroom.' He shook his head slowly from side to side. 'Why are you so afraid of me, Shelley?' he asked in a softer tone. 'I've never done you any harm. I certainly haven't meant to. What do you think I'm going to do? Attack you the minute we're alone? I've never had to resort to that, and believe me, I'm not about to start now.'

'Well——' she faltered, lowering her eyes in confusion.

But he wasn't through. 'You know what I think? I think you're actually afraid of yourself.'

She raised her chin. 'Don't be ridiculous!'

'Well,' he said with a shrug, 'it's the only explanation I can think of.' He paused. 'In any event, I'm not going to push it. It's entirely up to you.'

She really had no choice at this point. According to Blake's interpretation, if she didn't go it would look as though she didn't trust herself to be alone with him, meaning, of course, that she found him irresistible.

And he was right about one thing. There wasn't the slightest danger that he'd attack her or even try to pressure her. She believed him absolutely when he said he'd never resorted to strong-arm tactics. A man like Blake wouldn't have to!

Besides, she really did want to learn more about his plans for the paper. 'All right,' she said with a rather forced smile. 'I'm sorry. Let's go.'

His suite was on the first floor; it had a pleasant sitting-room with a couch and chair, a desk and small sideboard against one wall, a brick fireplace on another, with a wood fire already laid out. When they got inside, he switched on the lamp beside the couch, then took off his overcoat and turned to her.

'Why don't you take off your coat and sit down?' he said. 'I'll light the fire, then see what I have in the way of drinks.'

Shelley removed her own heavy coat and sat down gingerly on the edge of the couch, watching him as he got down on his haunches in front of the fireplace. As he lit the kindling, it flared up quickly, casting a bright glow on his strong features. He poked at it for a while until the heavy log on top caught fire, then got up and went over to the sideboard where a few bottles and glasses sat, shedding his jacket and loosening his tie along the way.

'What would you like?' he called to her. He laughed. 'Scotch and soda or Scotch and water?'

'Water would be fine.'

'Now,' he said, coming back to sit beside her and handing her a glass, 'here's what I have in mind for the paper.'

She was still a little wary of him and more than a little nervous about being alone with him like this, but after a few sips of her drink, watching the steady, silent snowfall through the window, the pleasant warmth of the fire, she began to thaw out.

For the next hour or so they discussed his plan in some detail, and by the time he'd finished and she'd asked all the questions she could think of at the moment it began to seem more and more feasible to her. In fact, it could solve everything.

'Of course,' she said at last, 'I'll have to discuss the whole thing with Dad. I don't know what his feelings are about it.'

'Certainly,' he replied promptly. 'He seemed agreeable enough the few times he and I have discussed it, but he thinks very highly of your judgement, and your opinion will make a difference. He's very pleased, you know, that you've taken such an interest. In fact, I had the feeling that he's hoping you plan to stay on.' After a brief hesitation he said, 'Are you?'

'I think so,' she answered slowly. 'I enjoy the work, so far anyway, even aside from helping Dad.' She smiled. 'He always wanted me to go into the paper with him. I was probably foolish not to, the way things turned out.' She bit her lip, suddenly aware that she'd said more than she meant to.

'Oh, I don't know,' Blake said casually, leaning back and stretching out his long legs. 'We all need our share of experience, it seems, and the more unpleasant it is, the quicker we learn from it, the more thorough the lesson.' He rested his arm along the back of the couch and leaned a little closer to her. 'I take it you're over all that at last,' he said quietly. 'At least you seem to have recovered nicely.'

She looked away, still hesitant to discuss it. Then, on a sudden impulse, she turned back to him and gave him a direct look. 'You were right, you know— I mean about Jim. He was only using me.'

He held her eyes in his for a long moment, and as she searched the blazing blue depths, trying to fathom what lay behind them, she was relieved to discover that she couldn't see a trace of pity there. If anything, what she saw was approval, even admiration.

He shook his head slowly. 'I always knew the man was a born schemer, a clever manipulator,' he said in a dead serious voice. 'And what he did to you only proved it.' He laughed to break the tension. 'Although, to be honest, I'll have to admit he's turned out to be a fine governor.'

Shelley had to laugh with him. 'Well, that's something. And I guess we should give the devil his due.'

Once again her eyes met his, and this time there was a softer glow in them, a barely concealed hunger, and the laughter died on her lips. Under that silent scrutiny a slow warmth began to fill her, and when he reached out a hand to place it on her cheek she drew in a sharp breath, but for the life of her couldn't move.

Suddenly, in a flash, it all came back to her— the times they'd spent together, what good company he was, how he'd gone out of his way to please her, how he'd pursued her so persistently when he could have had any woman he wanted. And she remembered, too, how attracted she'd been to him even when she'd imagined she was so in love with Jim Carruthers.

In fact, without Jim standing between them, she could see Blake now in an entirely new light. She should be flattered that this devastating man had sought her out again, that he still wanted her, even in the face of her flat rejections of him in the past.

In the next moment he had reached out for her. Instinctively, without a thought, she threw her arms around his neck, clinging to him, pressing herself up against his hard, muscular chest, and buried her head in his shoulder.

# CHAPTER SEVEN

'OH, GOD, Shelley,' Blake breathed in her ear, 'you don't know how long I've wanted to hold you like this.'

After a moment he raised his head and put a hand under her chin, forcing it around so that she was facing him. Then slowly his head came down. She closed her eyes, waiting, and when his lips met hers, she seemed to go limp inside. He kissed her then, a long, lingering kiss that set her pulses racing, her heart pounding.

As the kiss became more urgent, his tongue pushing past her parted lips, filling the interior of her mouth, one large hand moved to rest on her cheek, then moved to clasp her gently around the neck. It rested there at the base of her throat for a moment, then slid slowly downwards until it settled on her breast.

Mindlessly, she arched her back, revelling in his touch, and as the hand began to move slowly, sensuously across the silky fabric of her blouse, lingering over each taut thrusting peak, she felt she would go mad with desire.

He tore his mouth away from hers and buried his head in her hair. 'I want you, Shelley,' he gasped. At the same time, the hand at her breast slid inside the loose opening of her blouse, his fingers gliding over the soft bare flesh underneath. Gradually he pressed forward, easing her back on

the couch so that she was half lying down, her head
on the armrest. She looked up at him to see that
one dark lock of hair had fallen over his forehead.
Smiling, she reached up to smooth it back.

Obviously encouraged by the intimate gesture,
Blake removed his hand and started to unfasten the
buttons of her blouse. When he'd done that, he
spread the openings apart and gazed down with a
look of intense longing on his face at the sight of
the wispy bra, all that covered her now.

Then he left her for a moment to unbutton his
shirt quickly and shrug out of it. She watched,
entranced, as the bare expanse of tanned flesh and
the broad muscular shoulders were gradually revealed, then couldn't stop herself from reaching out
her hands to run them down over the smooth skin.

He groaned deep in his throat and reached down
to fumble with the front fastening of her bra. When
he'd unhooked it he put his hands on her shoulders
to raise her up to a sitting position, holding her so
that their bare flesh was just touching. After a
moment, he moved back slightly to cup each high,
firm mound in a hand, as though weighing the
fullness, his thumbs making circles around the hard
tips, until she was aching with longing.

He bent his head then to press his lips in the valley
between her breasts, and when his mouth moved
from one to the other Shelley threw her head back,
lost in a pleasure that was almost painful in its in-
tensity. With his mouth still at her breast, his
hand slid down her body to her thighs, but when
the hand reached up under her skirt she
stiffened involuntarily.

Clearly they were rapidly approaching the point of no return. If she didn't stop him now it would be too late. She put a hand on his, halting the upward exploration, and he raised his eyes to give her a searching look.

'Shelley?' he rasped harshly. 'Is something wrong?'

'I—I'm not sure,' she stammered. 'I——'

Just then the telephone shrilled into the silence of the room. Blake jerked his head up, a scowl darkening his features. Shelley seized the opportunity to move slightly away from him and hastily started straightening her skirt and buttoning up her blouse. The telephone continued to ring.

'What are you doing?' he demanded sharply. 'If you think I'm going to stop now and answer that damned phone...'

'You have to,' she said, forcing her voice to sound steady. 'It might be my parents. They'll be worried about me, wondering if something happened.'

Muttering under his breath a stream of invective that Shelley was grateful she couldn't quite make out, he got up, strode over to the still ringing telephone and snatched it off the hook.

'Yes?' he barked. 'What is it?' He listened for a moment, still frowning, then said in an icy tone, 'No, I won't take the call. And I don't want any more calls put through tonight at all.'

After he had hung up, he stayed there beside the telephone with his hand still on the receiver for several long seconds, his head bowed, as though deep in thought.

'Blake?' Shelley called. 'What is it?'

He turned and gave her a rueful smile. 'Just the newspaper, tracking me down. Nothing important.'

She watched as he crossed over to the window and pulled the curtain aside. He stood there silently peering out into the darkness, one hand rubbing slowly over the back of his neck. Something was obviously bothering him, and when she got up to join him at the window she could see immediately what it was.

The snow was coming down harder than ever, covering everything in sight. Down below in the front drive she could see her car, a thin white layer already blanketing the hood. It was also sticking to the road now that the temperature had dropped, with soft drifts piling up at the sides. It was eerily silent, with not another car in sight.

Blake put an arm lightly around her shoulders and gave her a little squeeze. 'Much as I hate to admit it,' he said in a low tone of regret, 'I think you'd probably better get home while you can still drive safely in this stuff. It'll freeze over before long, and you could get stuck.'

Her heart sank. The last thing she wanted was to leave him now, just when they were getting their past differences ironed out and finally beginning to understand each other. Why couldn't she forget about driving home and simply stay the night with him? She looked up at him, about to suggest it.

But as though he could read her mind he was shaking his head sadly from side to side. 'I know what you're thinking,' he said carefully, 'and please don't tempt me. My chivalrous instincts only go so far. It's a small town, remember? Appearances must be maintained.'

She knew he was right, and although she was disappointed she could barely contain her laughter at the look of chagrin on his face.

He eyed her narrowly. 'It's not funny!' he exclaimed stoutly. 'You're looking at a man in pain.'

She put a hand on his cheek. 'Oh, you'll survive,' she said, still teasing. But when she saw the sudden glint in his eyes she dropped her hand quickly and turned from him to retrieve her handbag. 'Now,' she went on in a brusque voice, 'if I'm going to leave I'd better do it now.'

'All right,' he said with a deep heartfelt sigh. 'But it's not going to end here. You know that, don't you?'

She nodded. 'Yes,' she replied softly, 'I know that.'

Later that night, lying in bed, the taste of Blake's kisses still on her mouth, the memory of his touch still warming her, Shelley knew she was lost. She'd behaved entirely out of character, responding to him so ardently, and still couldn't quite understand how it had happened. All she knew was that for the first time in years a man had awakened passion in her that she thought was dead forever. The great love she thought she'd felt for Jim Carruthers paled in comparison.

Then, just as she was about to drop off to sleep, it hit her with a sharp jab of fear that made her blood run cold. Her eyes flew open and she sat bolt upright.

She was in love with him! But how could that be? And how could it have happened so fast? He was clearly a man determined to stay footloose, free

of commitment, and there certainly was no hope
of a future with him.

And how would the proposed deal with her father
affect the situation? Perhaps it would be better to
try to talk him out of it. On the other hand, if it
went through, chances were she and Blake would
be thrown together more, and perhaps he'd change
his mind about a permanent relationship.

In the end, she knew she had to put aside her
own personal feelings and do what would be best
for her father. It was the only way she could live
with herself. If she was to have any kind of a future
with Blake, it couldn't be at the expense of her
father's health and well-being.

The next morning at breakfast, Shelley tackled her
father about the sale of the paper. She had thought
hard about it during the long sleepless night, and
finally come to the conclusion that Blake's plan
made sense, that it was a wise move on its own
merits, by far the best solution from her father's
point of view, regardless of how it would affect her
personally.

She waited until her mother had served them the
usual bacon and eggs, then left to go and bath and
dress. Although Shelley trusted her judgement
about personal issues, her presence during a purely
business discussion would only muddy the waters.

When she was safely out of earshot, Shelley
turned to her father, as usual totally absorbed in
the morning paper. 'Dad,' she said quietly.

'Hmm?' he replied abstractedly from behind the
sports page.

'Dad,' she went on a little more loudly, 'I'd like to know how you really feel about Blake's offer to buy you out.'

Slowly he lowered the paper, then sat gazing thoughtfully at her for a few moments, eyes twinkling behind his glasses. 'Ah, so it's Blake, is it? Pretty chummy, considering you just met the man yesterday.' He laughed. 'That must have been some ride last night!'

Reddening, Shelley lowered her eyes and took a hasty swallow of coffee. 'Well,' she finally said, setting her cup down carefully and meeting his quizzical gaze, 'to be perfectly honest, we had met before.'

'Ah, I see,' was all he said, nodding owlishly.

'It wasn't meant as a deception,' she rushed on. 'I'm sure you know by now that the whole episode with Jim Carruthers and my work on his campaign turned out to be pretty unpleasant for me. Blake was somewhat involved. Only peripherally,' she added quickly. 'But when I saw him here yesterday it only reminded me of things I wanted to forget, and at the time it just seemed better to act as though we'd never met.'

'I see. And now?'

She shrugged. 'Well, we had a long talk last night, and I came away half convinced it might work out for the best all around if you did decide to sell. I mean, considering the fact that you really should take it a little easier now.'

'Are you trying to tell me you don't want to stay and work with me?' he asked softly. He held up a hand, stopping her before she could answer. 'I'm only asking,' he went on. 'You know I'd never try to tie you here against your will. I've had my life; yours is still ahead of you. As far as the paper is concerned, you must do what's best for you.'

'No,' she declared stoutly, 'it's not that at all. I love working on the paper. But I'm still very green, and have an awful lot to learn. It just seemed to me that if Blake's company took over the business end it would leave you free to teach me so that I could work into it gradually.'

Her father heaved a deep sigh and got up to pour himself another cup of coffee. 'Well, much as I hate to admit it, you're probably right. I don't want to give up control entirely, but if what this fellow claims is true he'd still give me a free hand with editorial policy.' He sat back down across from her and gave her a direct look. 'You know him. Can he be trusted?'

Shelley searched her mind for a way to answer him. Could Blake be trusted? Her past dealings with him flashed through her mind. While she still had lingering doubts about trusting him on a personal basis, from what she knew of him, his professional behaviour was beyond reproach.

'Yes,' she said at last, 'I'm convinced that in any business dealing he'd be the soul of integrity, and that if he presents you with a proposal you can believe he'll come through with what he promises.'

'Well, that's good enough for me,' he told her. 'Then I guess the next step is to set up a meeting with him to discuss his terms in more detail. Since you've dealt with him in the past, I'd like you to be there too. In fact, you might as well call him right away and see if we can't get together some time today.' He chuckled. 'There's never much in the way of news the day after Thanksgiving anyway, and Stella's there to answer the telephone.'

Shelley scraped her chair back and stood up. 'All right. Any particular time?'

'Why don't you invite him for lunch?'

She laughed. 'Shouldn't we consult Mother about that first?'

'I don't think it's necessary,' he replied with a knowing smile. 'She's already so smitten with the man that we could tell her he's moving into the house permanently, and she'd be delighted.'

'All right, then, if you're sure.'

She started walking out of the kitchen, but when she reached the door to the hall she heard him call to her again and turned around to face him. His face was slightly troubled.

'Shelley, just one more thing,' he said slowly. 'You said just now that he could be trusted, but then you qualified it right away, and I gathered that you weren't so sure about him on a personal level. Now, it's been my experience that if a man will betray a personal confidence he can't be trusted in business either.'

As Shelley mulled this over, she realised that her statement had probably been misleading. 'I'm sorry, Dad,' she said at last. 'That just slipped out. From what I know of Blake, he doesn't make promises he doesn't intend to keep on any level.'

He nodded, reassured. 'Then you'd better make that call,' he said, and went back to his sports page.

Just as she reached the telephone in the front hall, Shelley looked up to see that her mother was coming down the stairs. She was fresh from her bath and dressed neatly as always, but Shelley noticed that her shoulders were slumped and her face grey with worry.

'I'm about to call Blake Fowler,' Shelley called to her. 'Dad wants to invite him to lunch so we can talk over his offer to buy the paper. Will that be all right with you?'

Immediately her mother's whole face lit up. She even stood a little straighter, as though a great weight had been lifted from her shoulders, and Shelley knew she'd done the right thing.

'Oh, of course,' her mother replied, hurrying down the last few steps to come to Shelley's side. 'I take it you've convinced him to sell,' she went on, her voice pitched low. 'I'm so glad, darling. It's been such a worry to me.'

Shelley laughed. 'Well, I don't know if I've convinced him to sell, but I think I've reassured him he can trust Blake. I only hope I'm right.'

Her mother's eyes flew open. 'Why, of course you're right. All you have to do is talk to Blake for five minutes to see that he's a man of honour. You go ahead and call him, and I'll go see what I can find to fix for lunch. I wonder what he likes?' she murmured, moving towards the kitchen.

'Just about everything, would be my guess,' Shelley replied.

She looked up the number of the inn, dialled, then when the clerk answered asked for Blake's room. While she waited, she offered up a little prayer that she really was doing the right thing. Her mother's whole-hearted approval carried a lot of weight.

'Hello,' came the familiar voice, crisp and businesslike.

'Blake, it's Shelley.'

'Ah, Shelley,' he said, his voice immediately gentling into a more intimate tone. 'How are you this morning?'

'I'm fine. Listen, Blake, my father asked me to call to set up a meeting with you about your offer. Can you come here for lunch today?'

'Certainly,' was the prompt reply. 'What time?'

'Oh, come at noon. I haven't even looked outside yet. I hope the driving conditions are better than they were last night.'

'Actually, they're much worse—it froze solid during the night. But it doesn't matter. I'd intended to walk in any case. I'll see you around twelve, then.'

The meeting went off far better than Shelley could have anticipated. She'd been expecting her father to balk at some of Blake's terms, but in the end it was clearly a case of two fair-minded men who saw a mutual advantage in the arrangement, so that by three o'clock that afternoon it was all decided, and the two men shook hands on their final agreement.

They were in John Dalton's study, a fire blazing on the hearth, sitting in comfortable chairs around a low table scattered with notes they'd taken, figures arrived at, future plans outlined.

'Well, now,' John said, rising to his feet. 'This calls for a little celebration. I'll just go get the sherry and some glasses. Be right back.'

When he was gone, Blake turned to Shelley. 'Well,' he said, 'what do you think?'

'I think you've got yourself another newspaper,' she replied with a smile.

'That wasn't what I meant. How do you feel, personally, about it? I know you had reservations when we first discussed it.'

'Well, believe me, I never would have tried to talk my father into it if my doubts hadn't been satisfied. I think it's the best thing for him, and that's really all that matters.'

'And what about you? Can you live with it? A lot depends on your willingness to stay here and help him.'

'Well, since I intended to do that anyway, this only makes it that much easier for me.'

John Dalton came back just then with drinks, his wife right behind him, beaming broadly at the news that the deal was finalised. The four of them drank a toast to the new partnership, then Blake set his glass down, refusing a refill.

'I'll have to go back to Seattle right away to consult with my board of directors and our attorneys. Then I'll get the paperwork drawn up. In the meantime, John, you'll no doubt want to consult your own attorney.'

Shelley's heart sank. Somehow she hadn't realised that when an agreement was reached Blake would no longer have any reason to stay in town. It had all happened so fast that that fact had simply passed her by. Was it all going to end so soon? Would she never even see him again? After last night, her hopes for some kind of relationship with him had been raised. Were they all to come to nothing now that his business was completed?

She looked at him now, still talking with her father, and what she was feeling must have shown on her face, because her mother's voice suddenly broke in.

'John, now that it's all settled, I think it's time you had your rest,' she announced firmly. 'You know what the doctor said.'

He opened his mouth, a protest clearly in mind, but something in his wife's expression stopped him, and it snapped shut. 'Yes, dear,' he said meekly, and started following her out of the room.

When her parents were gone, there was a heavy silence in the room, with only the crackle of the fire to break the stillness. Shelley stood there for a moment, staring into the flames, unable to think of how to say goodbye to Blake, when suddenly, in three long strides, he was at her side.

'Shelley,' he said in a low voice.

She looked up at him. 'Yes?'

He put a hand under her chin, his face grave. 'I'm coming back, you know.'

Immediately the burden on her heart lifted. 'You are?'

'Of course I am, silly,' he said in a teasing voice. 'After last night you don't think I'm just going to fade out of the picture, do you? You and I have some unfinished business to settle between us, and once this agreement is signed, sealed and delivered we're going to take up exactly where we left off.'

'Exactly?' she said, gazing into his eyes with a smile.

Their eyes locked together for a long moment, then Blake reached out for her and she leaned into him, her arms snaking around his waist as he held her close.

'Well, I have to admit I'm hoping for some progress in that direction,' he murmured.

He kissed her then, a long sweet kiss that melted away all her reservations about him. He was coming back soon. That was all she needed to know.

Sadly, however, Shelley's euphoria didn't last long. Blake hadn't been gone two days before her old doubts about him began to rise up to haunt her. What was he doing? Who was he with? He wasn't a man who would be without female companionship for long.

She kept repeating to herself as a kind of litany He said he'd be back, and she believed him. But what did that really mean? Once the negotiations for the purchase of the paper were over with, he'd probably just disappear out of her life. She had no intention of leaving town now, and his life was definitely in the city.

Then, too, his last words to her kept nagging at the back of her mind. What was the 'progress' he was hoping for in their relationship? It was what she wanted too, but somehow she had a sinking feeling that their definitions of the word weren't quite the same, that while to her progress meant a movement towards something lasting, to him it meant the consummation of what would turn out to be a brief affair.

By the time he called her, then, all her old defences against him were firmly in place. Although the sound of his voice could still make her heart pound and her knees go weak, she deliberately raised her guard up to put a distance between them.

'Oh, hello, Blake,' she said coolly.

'I just called to check in,' he said. 'I wanted to let you know that the paperwork should be completed in a few days.'

'So soon?' she queried. 'I thought it would take at least another week or two.'

He laughed. 'Well, I'll have to admit I've done some prodding to get things moving a little faster. How are things going at your end? Has John had any second thoughts?'

'No, he's convinced he's doing the right thing. He trusts you, too.'

'Well, good. With luck, I could make it up by the weekend.'

'Fine. I know he'll be glad to get it settled.'

There was a short silence. 'Shelley?' he said at last in a puzzled voice. 'Is something wrong?'

'No, of course not,' she replied. 'I'm just anxious to get this whole thing settled.'

'Why is that?' he asked lightly. 'I hope it isn't because you think you'll be rid of me then.'

Although his tone was casual, even flippant, there was an undercurrent of seriousness in it that warmed her heart. Maybe it wouldn't end when his business with her father was over. It could even be that his intentions were quite serious where she was concerned. Did she dare hope?

'No,' she said slowly at last. 'Of course not.'

'Good,' came the firm reply. 'Then hold that thought until I see you again. I'll try to make it by Saturday. If not, I'll call and let you know.' He paused for a moment, then went on in a lower, more intimate voice, 'I've missed you, Shelley.'

Her heart caught in her throat. 'I'm glad,' she said happily. 'Me too.'

'Until Saturday, then,' he said.

After they'd hung up Shelley stood there for a long time, her hand still on the receiver, tears of happiness rising unbidden to her eyes. Blake *did* care! He missed her, and in just a few days she'd see him again.

When Saturday came Shelley spent the entire morning, from the moment she got up, on pins and needles, counting the hours, even the minutes, until he showed up. He hadn't called again, so that had to mean he'd be arriving some time today as planned. It was a three-hour drive from Seattle, and since they hadn't had any more snow the roads were in good condition.

As it turned out, he arrived shortly before noon, putting her out of her misery. She was in the kitchen helping her mother prepare lunch when she heard the crunch of tyres in the gravel driveway. She dropped the lettuce she was breaking for salad into the bowl and ran to the window.

He was just getting out of his car, reaching inside for his briefcase, and the sight of him in his dark windbreaker, so tall and strong, his face reddened slightly by the cold, his breath visible in the frosty air, his dark hair ruffled by the strong breeze, was enough to take her breath away. If she'd ever had any doubts that she was already hopelessly in love with him, seeing him now made them evaporate into thin air.

Forcing herself to be calm, taking slow, deliberate steps, she walked to the door and opened it. Just then he raised his head, and their eyes met across the short distance that separated them. He grinned broadly and came striding towards her, his arms outstretched. She stumbled towards him and fell against him, and as his arms came around her she knew everything would be all right now.

'Come inside,' she said, releasing herself and taking him by the hand. 'You're just in time for lunch.'

That afternoon the four of them, Blake, Shelley and both her parents, drove into town to visit John's lawyer. After a careful examination of the papers Blake's legal advisers had prepared, and making only a few minor changes, the agreement was signed, and Blake's company became the new owners of John's newspaper.

'This calls for a celebration,' John said as they were driving home. 'Let's all go out for dinner tonight at the inn.'

'No,' his wife put in firmly, taking him by the arm. 'It's already five o'clock and you haven't had your afternoon rest. We'll celebrate at home and you'll get to bed early. Besides, I have our dinner all planned.' She turned to Blake. 'You'll join us, I hope?'

'Thanks,' he replied. 'I'd like that. Right now, after I drop you off, I should go check in at the inn and get settled. Then I need to make a few calls, let the powers that be in Seattle know that the deal is finalised.'

'Well, we'll expect you for dinner when you're through. Say around six-thirty? Will that give you enough time?'

'Sounds about right.' He glanced at Shelley and gave her a warm smile. 'I'll see you later, then.'

That evening the elder Daltons retired soon after dinner, leaving Blake and Shelley together in the

living-room. It was the first time she'd been alone
with him all day, and she was feeling a little shy of
him, still wondering too if now that the sale was
finalised he would fade out of the picture.

They sat side by side on the couch, sipping their
after-dinner drinks, watching the flickering flames
of the fire Blake had built earlier, and listening to
the sound of her parents moving around upstairs
as they got ready for bed.

When there was finally only silence to be heard
from that quarter, Blake turned to her and took her
hand in his, shifting his body around so that he
faced her. He reached out to run a hand over her
hair, which fell loosely to her shoulders.

'God, I missed you, Shelley,' he said in a low
voice. 'There was hardly a moment I didn't think
about you, about the last time we were together.'

With his words, all her reservations vanished. She
looked deeply into his eyes, and the desire gleaming
there in the blazing blue depths intensified her own
longing. The heat building up between them was
palpable, and when he took her in his arms she fell
against him with a heartfelt sigh. Then his head
came down, and as his mouth claimed hers she gave
herself up to him with a sigh of deep contentment.

His hands began to move feverishly over her
body, and his mouth opened wider, his tongue
pushing past her eager lips. One hand had just
moved to her breast and was slipping inside the
loose opening of her dress when suddenly the sound
of her mother's voice was heard, calling her from
upstairs, breaking the spell.

'Shelley,' it came again.

They broke apart slowly. Rolling her eyes and shrugging, she smoothed down her skirt, rose to her feet and went out into the hall. Her mother was at the top of the stairs leaning over the banister, gazing down at her with an apologetic smile.

'I'm so sorry to bother you, dear, but I had to make sure you'd remember to lock the doors before you go to bed.'

'Yes, Mother, I'll remember.'

With a sigh, Shelley turned to go back to the living-room, but before she'd gone far Blake came walking towards her, a frown of frustration on his lean features.

'I think I might as well go now,' he said. 'This won't do.' He put his hands on her shoulders and looked down into her eyes. 'I don't suppose I can talk you into coming back to the inn with me?'

She laughed shakily, sorely tempted. 'Afraid not. Remember it's a——'

'Yes, I know,' he broke in drily. 'It's a small town.' He thought a moment. 'I'll tell you what—let's go for a drive tomorrow. As a matter of fact, the company is thinking about buying a nearby ski lodge, and I said I might look into it while I was up here. We could make a day of it. Just the two of us,' he added with feeling.

'Oh, yes,' she agreed quickly, 'I'd like that.'

'Fine. We should get an early start. How about if I pick you up around nine o'clock?'

'That sounds great. I'll be ready.'

With one last lingering kiss, he was gone.

After she'd closed the door and locked it, Shelley leaned back against it, smiling happily to herself.

Tomorrow she'd have a whole day alone with him. What was more, if he was going to explore the possibility of purchasing a ski lodge in the area, it could mean that he just might be considering a permanent move.

# CHAPTER EIGHT

THE next day dawned bright and clear, perfect weather for a drive up into the nearby ski area. The lodge Blake wanted to look over was only a two-hour drive, but they got a later start than they'd planned on, then stopped for a long, leisurely lunch halfway there, so that it was mid-afternoon before they arrived.

With the recent thaw the skiing conditions still weren't good enough to attract much business at the lodge, so they had the place virtually to themselves. They were met by the manager, who conducted them on a tour of the grounds and the lodge itself.

When they'd seen everything Blake was interested in, they came back to the lobby, where a fire was blazing in an enormous stone fireplace. There was a smattering of guests by now, all in ski apparel and lounging in the comfortable chairs before the fire.

'Well, Mr Fowler,' the manager said as he led them inside, 'that just about covers it, but if you have any questions I'll be glad to answer them. No doubt you'll want to inspect our books before you make a decision, though.'

'Oh, I'll have our accounting people do that,' Blake replied. 'And thank you for your time. I think I've seen enough to make a report to my board. I don't know, of course, what the final decision will be, but I must say I'm favourably impressed.'

'Ah, good,' the manager said. He stepped behind the front desk, took out a key from a slot and handed it to Blake. 'Your room is all ready if you want to freshen up before dinner. There's a fire laid out, and you can order from room service, if you prefer. Would you like someone to show you the way?'

'No, thanks. We can find it.'

Shelley stood there rooted to the spot, staring at the two men. His room? What did that mean? When Blake turned to her she gave him a questioning look, but he only took her by the arm and began walking towards the long corridor that led to the guest rooms.

'Er—Blake,' she said, holding back a little, 'what's this about a room?'

'Oh, the company reserved one for me,' he replied with an offhand shrug. 'We might as well take advantage of it.'

Still not quite satisfied, she went along with him down the hall until he found the right door. He unlocked it and stood back. Cautiously she stepped inside. It was a large room with another smaller stone fireplace, a table and two comfortable chairs in front of it, a bulky oak armoire and two dressers. And, over in an alcove, a wide double bed.

She looked at Blake, who was shrugging out of his heavy jacket. Still a little uneasy, she walked slowly over to the window that overlooked the ski slope and stood there looking out at the snow-covered mountainside, the tall evergreens in the background almost black against the sparkling white blanket.

It was such a beautiful scene, and so peaceful, that she soon became lost in the wonderful sense of awe and well-being that came from closeness to nature's grandeur.

In a moment she heard Blake come up behind her, felt his hands on her shoulders, tugging at her jacket. He slipped it off, tossed it on a nearby chair, then came back to her, and when his arms came around her, enfolding her, she leaned back against him. He bent his head down to press his cheek against hers, the slight stubble rasping sensuously on her skin.

At that moment she felt such an intense surge of happiness at being entirely alone with the man she loved in such a lovely setting that her last doubt vanished and she simply gave herself up to the sheer enjoyment of the moment.

Smiling, she turned her head slightly towards him. Immediately his lips sought hers, and his hands slid down to cover her breasts. At the touch, her bloodstream seemed to catch fire and her knees grew weak. Drawing in her breath sharply, her eager lips still pressed against his, she eased her body around so that she was facing him. As she raised her arms up around his neck the kiss deepened, his tongue pushing inside her mouth, his hard lower body grinding into hers, his hands sliding now under her jersey, stroking the bare skin beneath.

After a moment, he raised his head and gazed down at her. 'Alone at last,' he said with a quirky smile, and with his arm around her shoulders began to lead her towards the bed.

It wasn't until they were halfway there that it suddenly hit her what she was about to do, and she stopped short. 'Blake,' she said in a small voice, 'I'm not sure I'm ready for this.'

He gave her a puzzled look. 'What do you mean? I thought it's what we both wanted.'

'Well, not exactly.' She shrugged. 'I mean, it's kind of sudden, isn't it? Shouldn't we talk about it?'

'What's there to talk about?' he asked, frowning now. He placed his hands on either side of her face. 'I'm crazy about you, Shelley—surely you know that?' He smiled and dropped one hand to brush it lightly over her breast. 'I've never wanted a woman the way I want you.'

She gazed up into his eyes, still dubious. She was tempted. She couldn't help herself, looking at him now with the shaft of sunlight coming in through the window blazing on his dark hair, the bright blue eyes glittering at her with such naked desire.

She looked away, biting her lip, her mind racing. What would be the harm? He wanted her, and she wanted him. She was no blushing virgin, but a mature woman who'd been married once. Above all, she loved him, helplessly, totally, with her whole being.

Yet she suddenly realised in a flash that it was the very depth of that love that made her hesitate now. To embark on an affair with Blake wouldn't prove her love, it would debase it. Love meant a total giving, mind and body, not indulgence in the thrill of the moment. That would only cheapen what to her was sacred.

'I'm sorry, Blake,' she said at last, stepping away from him and crossing her arms over her chest. 'I can't.'

He ran a hand through his hair in a gesture of sheer frustration. 'But why not?' he demanded. 'If you're trying to tell me you don't want me——'

'No,' she broke in, 'it's not that. You know it's not that.' She gazed up at him again, her eyes clouded with misery. 'It just seems—I don't know—wrong, somehow.'

'My God, woman!' he exclaimed heatedly, throwing up his hands and fixing her with a bewildered look. 'This isn't the Dark Ages! And you're not an innocent babe in the woods. Surely since your marriage you've had some romantic adventures?'

She smiled tremulously and lifted her chin. 'Actually, I haven't.'

He stared down at her, his eyes wide, incredulous. 'What about Jim Carruthers?'

Slowly she shook her head. 'No. Not even Jim.'

'Well, if that doesn't beat all!' Then he threw his head back and broke into peals of helpless laughter.

As she watched him, practically doubled up by now with hilarity—at her expense—a slow anger began to boil up within her, and her face went up in flame.

'I don't see what's so funny,' she declared stoutly when he'd simmered down a little. She pointed an accusing finger at him. 'You always do that.'

'Do what?' he asked, still chuckling.

'Make fun of me when I'm trying to be serious.' She put her hands on her hips and glared up at him. 'Just tell me what's so wonderful about hopping from bed to bed so casually the way you do, then maybe I'll be able to see the humour in *that*!'

The laughter died on his lips and he drew himself up to his full six feet plus height. 'I do not hop!' he commented sternly.

'Oh, no? Well, that isn't what I've heard. And if you think I'm going to be the next notch in your bedpost, you've got another think coming. Now, I'd like to go home, if you don't mind. My parents are expecting me back tonight.'

'You sound just like an adolescent girl,' he commented nastily. 'What do you think they'd do if you did stay out all night? Ground you for a few weeks?'

'No,' she snapped. 'They'd worry, that's what they'd do.'

'You could call them,' he said in a hopeful voice.

'And tell them what?' she demanded. 'Sorry, folks, I won't be home tonight, I'm spending the night with Blake?' She shook her head. 'No, Blake, it's just not on. Now, are you going to take me home, or shall I go down and check on the bus schedules?'

'You're behaving like a child,' he said. 'An unreasonable child at that, hanging on to an archaic moral code that has nothing to do with reality. This isn't a game, you know. You can't lead me on the way you've done, then just waltz away when you get cold feet.'

'Oh, can't I? And whose rule is that?' She gave him a long baleful look. 'You know, you've got some nerve, laughing at my moral values.'

He put his hands on his hips and looked down his nose at her. 'Oh? And what's that supposed to mean?' he asked, his voice steely.

'I'll tell you what it means,' she retorted, really angry by now, reckless and uncaring of what she said or how he took it. 'It means that in reality you're the one with the adolescent values, not me. It means that you're basically a coward, so terrified of commitment that all you have on your mind where women are concerned is to get them into bed by the quickest route possible, then take off when you get tired of them.'

'Ah, so that's it!' he said on a triumphant note. 'It's commitment you're after. God, how sick I am of that word!'

'No doubt. I'm surprised you even know what it means.'

'Well, if it means I have to promise to marry every woman I'm attracted to, you can keep it!' he snarled. 'The divorce-rate doesn't need me adding to it. As you well know.'

That was a low blow, a direct hit. Shelley had never really got over the shame she'd felt at the failure of her marriage, and the hurtful reminder only escalated her fury. Trembling with rage, she stamped her foot, then whirled around and marched straight to the door, snatching up her jacket and handbag as she went.

'Where are you going?' he called after her.

'Anywhere!' she cried. 'Just so long as it's out of here.'

'Oh, come on, Shelley,' he said, striding over to her side and putting a hand on her arm. She shrugged it off angrily and reached for the door.

'I'm sorry,' he went on. 'I didn't mean anything personal by that remark. It just slipped out.'

She turned to eye him warily. He seemed contrite enough, and his anger seemed to be spent. At least he wasn't laughing at her.

'Come on,' he said again. 'I'll drive you home.'

The ride back to town was a strained silent one, with Blake staring straight ahead, stony-faced, while Shelley pressed herself against the door, as far away from him as she could get. Neither of them uttered a word until he pulled up in front of her parents' house. It was past six o'clock and quite dark, and by now all her own anger had leaked away. She only felt drained, empty inside, as though she'd just been through a terrible accident.

The minute Blake stopped the car, and while the motor was still running, she reached for the handle and opened the door. He made no move to stop her, and when she stepped out on to the pavement she hesitated a moment. Then she leaned down to peer inside at him. His jaw was set, his eyes hooded, and he gazed back at her with a hard, blank expression on his face.

'Well,' she said stiffly, 'I'll say goodnight.' He didn't respond by so much as the flicker of an eyebrow. She couldn't just let it end this way. She took a deep breath. 'Blake, I said some things today I shouldn't have, and I'm sorry.'

'It doesn't matter,' he replied, tight-lipped.

'Well, then.' With a sigh, she straightened up and slammed the door shut.

In the next second, the car shot away from the kerb with a squeal of tyres on the still slushy pavement. She stood there for a moment or two

watching until it disappeared around the corner.
Then with a heavy heart, her shoulders sagging, she
turned and started walking slowly up the path towards the house.

'Well, dear, did you have a good time today?' her
mother asked.

It was about an hour after Shelley had arrived
home, and they were in the kitchen preparing their
usual late Sunday night supper. Shelley had gone
straight to her room, had a long bath, a good cry,
and then decided she'd better put in an appearance
or her mother would know something was wrong.

'Oh, yes,' she replied, forcing out a smile.

Her mother didn't say anything more for a while,
but Shelley was uncomfortably aware of the
thoughtful looks directed her way from time to time
as she set the table.

It wasn't until they'd started dishing up the food
that her mother spoke again, her voice casual and
matter-of-fact. 'You know, dear, I've been thinking
a lot lately about your future.'

Shelley laughed. 'Oh, really? And what was your
conclusion?'

'Well, I think you're really the kind of woman
who should be married. Dad and I aren't getting
any younger, and I'd feel better to see you safely
settled.'

'Oh, Mother, I tried that once; it was a disaster.'

'Yes, but you were just a child when you married
David. And so was he. Now, Blake is a mature man,
and it seems to me——'

'No, Mother,' Shelley broke in firmly, 'you can forget that. Blake Fowler has no intention of marrying anyone.'

'Oh, I can hardly believe that. I've seen you together, the way you look at each other.' Her mother pursed her lips and nodded firmly to emphasise her point. 'It's as clear as day that he's in love with you.'

Shelley racked her brains to think of a way to tell her sheltered mother that love didn't mean the same thing nowadays as it had when she was young. Besides, Blake didn't love her—at least, he'd never said so. He *wanted* her badly, but had no more idea of making a permanent commitment than flying to the moon.

'Well, Mother,' she finally said, 'times have changed, you know.'

'Well, I know that!' was the tart reply. 'I don't live in a cave, after all. But I also know that Blake is a man of integrity and not the kind to toy with a woman's affections.'

Shelley laughed. 'Now what does that mean? He hasn't made any promises, if that's what "toying with affections" means. And he's made it quite clear that he's not going to.'

Her mother gave her a troubled look. 'Then I guess you're right. I really don't understand,' she said in a bewildered voice. 'It seems like an awful waste of time to me. I mean, what's the point of a relationship with a man at all if you know from the start it can't go anywhere?'

Shelley sighed. 'If I knew the answer to that one, Mother, I'd patent it and become a millionaire.'

\*     \*     \*

For Shelley, the next few days passed in a blur. She kept trying to put that last conversation with her mother out of her mind, but it had disturbed her more than she realised. Was she wasting her time on a man who couldn't—or wouldn't—commit? But what was she to do? She loved him!

When Monday passed without a word from Blake, then Tuesday, she began to become seriously alarmed. She went down to the newspaper with her father each day and managed to perform her work competently enough, but her heart wasn't in it.

Quite simply, she missed him. They'd both said unforgivable things to each other, deliberately wounding remarks, but as the hurt and anger faded from her mind what she came to regret most bitterly was her refusal to spend the night with him at the lodge, as he'd clearly expected. And probably, she had to admit, as she'd led him to believe she would.

What would have been the harm? She loved him. Why shouldn't she take what he was willing to offer, enjoy it while it lasted, then let him go when it was over? At least then she'd have some happy memories to look back on instead of this terrible regret, the awful suspicion that her foolish pride had kept her from taking advantage of the opportunity of a lifetime.

Neither of her parents had so much as mentioned Blake's name during those two long days, and from the worried looks they darted her way from time to time she had the feeling they were both walking on egg-shells around her, afraid to raise the subject, even though she went out of her way to appear cheerful and unconcerned.

Every time the telephone rang, at home or at the paper, she nearly jumped out of her skin. She even looked for him out on the streets, hoping she might see him. It was a small town; there weren't that many places he could hide.

When Wednesday came and she still hadn't heard from him, she couldn't bear it another moment. She'd finally had enough. It was noon. Stella, the secretary, and her father were both out to lunch, and she was alone in the office, sitting at her desk, head in hands, sunk in gloom and staring at the telephone, still hoping it might ring.

Suddenly she knew what she had to do. Before she could change her mind she snatched up the receiver and dialled the inn where Blake was staying. All he could do was refuse to talk to her or tell her he never wanted to see her again. At least the suspense would be over and she could get on with her life.

'Mountain View Inn,' came the clerk's voice.

'I'd like to speak to Mr Fowler,' she said. 'Blake Fowler.'

'One moment.' There was a short silence, then the clerk came back on the line. 'I'm sorry, Mr Fowler has checked out.'

'Checked out? When?'

'Let's see. Ah, yes, he left us late Sunday evening. If you care to leave a message, I'll be glad to forward it for you.'

'No,' Shelley faltered. 'No, thanks, that won't be necessary.'

Slowly she replaced the receiver in its cradle. He was gone. He'd left that very day, left without calling her, without any explanation, not even saying goodbye.

What should she do? What *could* she do? Well, she'd gone this far. She might as well go all the way. She got up and went over to the shelf where they kept the out-of-town telephone directories, pulled out the huge Seattle volume and turned the pages until she found the number for the *News-Tribune*. Then she carried it back to her desk, and with shaking fingers dialled the number.

'Seattle *News-Tribune*,' came the operator's curt voice.

'Blake Fowler, please.'

'One moment, please. I'll connect you with his office.'

She waited, in an agony of suspense, as the telephone clicked and burred in her ear for several long seconds. You'd think I was calling Mars, she grumbled to herself. And what was she going to say to him? She hadn't the foggiest idea. All she wanted was to hear the sound of his voice again.

Finally a human being came on the line. 'Mr Fowler's office,' came a crisp feminine voice.

'I'd like to speak to Mr Fowler,' Shelley said.

'I'm sorry, Mr Fowler is not available.'

'Well, can you tell me when he'll be available?' she asked with some asperity. 'I'm a personal friend of his.'

'Oh.' There was a short silence. 'I'm sorry. I really can't say. He's taken an extended leave of absence, and I don't know when he'll be back.'

'I see. Well, thanks anyway,' Shelley said, and hung up.

She knew there was no point asking where he was. He could be in Timbuktu for all she knew, and his secretary certainly wasn't going to tell her, even if she knew. Besides, it was clear by now that if he'd wanted to speak to her he would have let her know himself. It was over, and she might as well face it.

Although at first Shelley was certain her heart was irreparably broken, it did become easier in time. By dint of hard work and a determined effort to keep all thoughts of Blake out of her mind, she managed to get through Christmas, and by the New Year her broken heart seemed to be on the mend.

Then, one day in early January she was just pulling into the driveway after work when she noticed a strange car parked in front of the house, a long, low luxury model, so opulent that it verged on a limousine. In fact, when she got out of her car and started towards the house she could see a uniformed driver sitting in the front seat, leaning back, his cap over his head, obviously asleep.

Her heart lurched sickeningly. Could it possibly be Blake? But what would he be doing in such a car? She imagined he was a rich man, but he'd never gone in for that kind of show. Still, it was possible, and she quickened her step.

As soon as she was inside the house, she could hear voices coming from the living-room. Slowly, her heart pounding, her knees weak, she crept silently over to the entrance and peered inside. There, to her astonishment, sitting down with a drink in his hand and chatting easily with her parents, was Jim Carruthers!

'Jim!' she cried, going inside. 'What in the world are you doing here?'

He jumped to his feet. 'Ah, Shelley,' he said, beaming. 'How good to see you.'

He reached out his arms, and automatically she fell into them. In spite of their troubled past, the old habit of friendship and admiration she'd always felt for him was too strong to resist. He kissed her lightly on the cheek.

'But what in the world are you doing here?' she asked again, drawing back from him.

'I had to come up this way on some official business, and finished it a little ahead of schedule. Then, as I passed through town, I recalled that this was where your parents lived and decided to see if you were staying with them. And your mother was kind enough to invite me in to wait for you to come home from work.'

He flashed his most brilliant smile at Ruth Dalton, who was almost swooning with delight at entertaining the governor of the state in her own house. Shelley glanced hurriedly at her father, who she knew was not one of Jim's biggest fans. As she expected, the expression on his face was one of tolerant amusement, with just a tinge of cynicism.

'Oh, it's our pleasure entirely,' her mother gushed. 'It's a great honour to have the governor in our home.' She turned to Shelley. 'We've invited him for dinner, but he said he wanted to wait until you came to decide.'

Jim looked at Shelley, one eyebrow cocked enquiringly. 'Well? How about it, Shelley?' he asked in a low, more intimate tone. 'Am I welcome?'

Of course she knew exactly what he was referring to. The last time they'd seen each other was the night he'd announced his engagement to Vanessa Talbot, a betrayal of all he'd implicitly promised her. But since then Blake Fowler had come into her life, and she hadn't given Jim Carruthers another thought.

As she looked at him now, still handsome, still impressive-looking, every inch a governor, she couldn't imagine for the life of her how she ever could have thought she was in love with him. He certainly had no more power over her, and it would break her mother's heart if she missed this chance to entertain such a prominent figure.

'Of course you're welcome,' she said with a warm smile. 'But what about your poor driver out in the car? It's freezing cold.'

'Oh, I'll send him on to the inn now that I'm definitely staying for dinner.' Jim shrugged diffidently. 'I plan to spend a few days in the area.' He glanced over at John Dalton, who still hadn't uttered a word since Shelley came in. 'As you no doubt realise, this part of the state isn't exactly behind me, and I thought I might try to mend some fences.'

'Good idea,' her father snapped. 'There are a few issues I wouldn't mind discussing with you. For instance——'

'John,' his wife broke in firmly, 'would you mind coming out to the kitchen with me? I thought we might have that bottle of champagne we didn't drink at the New Year's party, and you'll have to open it for me.' She simpered at Jim. 'It's not every day we have such good reason to celebrate.'

Shelley smiled to herself as he got up out of his chair and followed his wife from the room, grumbling under his breath every step of the way.

When they were out of earshot, Jim turned to her, laughing. 'I gather I wasn't your father's favourite candidate.'

'Sorry about that,' Shelley replied. 'He's got some pretty firm ideas about the problems in the state and doesn't feel you addressed them to his satisfaction.'

'Well, maybe I can change his mind. Right now, I'd better go out and relieve my driver.' Jim took both her hands in his and gazed into her eyes. 'But don't go away,' he went on in a lower, more intimate voice. 'I really came to see you, Shelley. We have some unfinished business to take care of.'

He left her then, and while he was gone she went over to the sideboard to pour herself a glass of sherry. What in the world could he have meant by that remark? And where was Vanessa? He hadn't even mentioned her. She had to smile, wondering how the possessive blonde would react to the news that he'd come to visit her.

It was with a definite sense of *déjà vu* that Shelley drove Jim back to the inn that night after dinner, a repetition of exactly the same scenario with Blake just a month ago, except that it wasn't snowing.

Then, when she pulled up into the curving drive in front and he asked her to come in and have a drink with him, she couldn't suppress the laughter that escaped her lips at the uncanny replay.

'I don't see what you find so amusing,' he said, hurt. He eyed her carefully. 'You've changed, Shelley.'

'Oh? In what way?'

'I don't know. You seem—harder somehow. More self-assured.'

'That's not very flattering.'

'Oh, I didn't mean it as a criticism,' he assured her hastily. 'In fact, if anything, it adds to the attraction.' He paused then, as another car pulled up behind them, its headlights glaring through the rear window, 'Now, how about that drink?'

Shelley thought quickly. What would be the harm? She was immune to Jim's charm. There was no danger here. In a moment the car behind them would start to honk.

'All right,' she said, turning into a parking space, 'I'll have a drink with you.'

One departure from the previous scene was that Jim didn't make straight for his room the way Blake had. Instead, he led her into the small cocktail lounge off to one side of the lobby. It wasn't very crowded, and no one except the waiter seemed to recognise him.

They were seated in a dim corner at the back of the room, and after they'd ordered they sat there in silence, listening to the piano music tinkling softly in the background. It wasn't until their drinks arrived and Jim had taken a healthy swallow of his Scotch and soda that he turned to her, his expression grave, his eyes searching.

'I've thought about you so often these past few months,' he said in a low voice. 'In fact, I almost called you several times.'

He stopped and gave her a direct look, as though waiting for a response. Since she couldn't think of a thing to say, however, she only took a sip of her drink and gazed steadily at him over the rim of her glass. The ball was in his court. She wasn't going to help him out.

He frowned slightly and leaned back in his chair. 'I felt terrible over that whole episode—you know, about the engagement to Vanessa. I knew at the time I should have told you about it. It was unforgivable the way I just sprang it on you on election night. I didn't really grasp how it might have affected you, though, until you disappeared.'

He paused again, and this time she decided it was time to speak. 'How is Vanessa?' she asked quietly.

To her intense satisfaction, he flushed deeply and looked away. He gazed fixedly down at his drink, twirling the glass around in his hands in slow circles for a few moments, then finally heaved a sigh and raised his eyes to hers again.

'That's all off,' he mumbled.

'Really?' she said.

'I'm afraid so.'

She was taken completely by surprise. It occurred to her then that actually she'd never seen an announcement of his marriage in the newspaper, but during the past few months she'd been so involved with her own affairs, and so anxious to put the whole episode with Jim behind her, that she hadn't really paid any attention.

'I'm    sorry,    Jim,'    she    said    at    last. 'What happened?'

He shrugged. 'Let's just say it was mutual.' He gave a dry laugh. 'I think Vanessa was far more interested in becoming the wife of the governor of the state than of Jim Carruthers.' He reached out and placed a hand over hers. 'But there was a deeper reason.'

'And what was that?' she asked, suddenly uneasy.

'As soon as I realised you were gone for good, it really hit me what I'd lost in you. I need you, Shelley,' he went on in a low, pleading voice. 'I know it's presumptuous even to ask, but I can't help hoping that you'll be generous and forgive me. I was so caught up in my own ambition that I let go the best friend I had.'

'Of course I forgive you, Jim,' she replied promptly. 'I'll admit I was hurt at the time and that I had some vague hopes where you were concerned. I thought you really cared something about me, personally, but you hadn't actually said anything definite.' She smiled at him and gently withdrew her hand. 'But it's all water under the bridge now, ancient history. All I really want from you is that you be a good governor. That's what I worked so hard for, regardless of my personal feelings.'

He frowned. 'But I happen to want more than that,' he said firmly. 'After you left, it didn't take me long to discover that it was you I really cared about all the time. Your courage, your intelligence, your dedication, your loyalty.'

Shelley could only sit there staring at him, stunned. 'Jim,' she said at last, 'what is it you're trying to say to me?'

# CHAPTER NINE

WHILE Shelley waited for Jim's answer, she watched him carefully. Knowing him as well as she did, especially now that the scales of her old helpless love for him had fallen from her eyes, she could almost see the wheels turning around in his head, assessing the situation, her reaction to his words.

And, with a seasoned politician's sure instinct, he came up with just the right answer. 'For now,' he said carefully, 'just that we try to mend some old fences, get back on our old footing, before I ever decided to run for governor.'

'Isn't it a little late for that?' she asked softly. 'I'm still not clear what you have in mind, Jim, but I can tell you that there were aspects to that "old footing" you mentioned that I really wouldn't care to repeat.'

'Yes, yes, I know,' he assured her hastily. 'And I don't blame you in the slightest. I've already admitted I made a stupid blunder, an almost criminal error in judgement, in the way I treated you...' Here he broke off to give her his warmest, most sincere smile. 'I guess what I really want is that you let me try to make it up to you.'

'Jim, I already told you, there's no need...'

'Please,' he said, holding up a hand, 'let me tell you what I have in mind. As I mentioned earlier, I plan to stay around the area for a while. If you're willing, perhaps we can see each other, get re-acquainted on a more honest, open basis.'

Shelley leaned back in her chair, thinking it over for a few moments, and could come up with no compelling reason why she shouldn't do as he asked. Certainly a friend was better than an enemy, and there were still many things she admired about the man. There wasn't the slightest danger to her. She was immune to his charms now. And the distraction might get her mind off Blake.

'All right,' she said at last. 'I don't see any reason why we can't be friends.'

He nodded, obviously pleased. 'Good. That's all I ask.'

Jim stayed in town for five days, and during that time they were together almost constantly. He had scheduled several speeches in the neighbouring towns, and Shelley found time away from her work to accompany him on most of them. She enjoyed his company, felt quite comfortable with him. After all, they were old friends, had known each other for years.

Although he seemed to go out of his way to make her happy, he never pressed her for an answer or asked more of her in the way of lovemaking than an arm placed casually around her waist, a few friendly kisses on the cheek. With his unerring antennae, he seemed to realise instinctively that forcing any more intimate attentions on her would only make her balk.

Finally, it was time for him to leave. It was their last night together, and he took her out to dinner at a fine restaurant in a nearby town that was famous for its fresh seafood. During the meal, their conversation centred on his future plans. Clearly he was aiming for the Senate next, then after that who knew what giddy political heights he might scale?

It wasn't until they were back in front of Shelley's house that he broached the subject of their personal future. The heavy glass screen between the back seat and the driver was in place so that he could neither see nor hear, and the moment the motor was turned off Jim turned to her.

'Well,' he said, 'I'll be leaving tomorrow morning early, so I won't see you again. I've enjoyed these last several days, and I hope you have too.'

'Yes, I have. It's been fun.' She knew there was more to come, but couldn't really guess what it might be.

'Before I go, there's something I need to say to you,' he went on. He took her by the hand and gazed into her eyes. 'I love you, Shelley. I want you to marry me.'

Since she'd been half expecting something of the sort, she wasn't taken totally by surprise, but still she hadn't anticipated that he'd go quite that far or come out with it quite so baldly as that.

Her immediate reaction was that of course it was totally out of the question, but she couldn't quite bring herself to reject him as bluntly as all that. Old habits died hard, and, although there was no trace of her old helpless love for him left in her, there was still a lot to respect and admire about him.

'J-Jim,' she finally stammered, 'I don't know what to say. You've taken me completely by surprise.'

'Well, perhaps I was a little hasty,' he said, frowning, clearly rather annoyed that she hadn't jumped at the chance he was offering her. 'Let me ask you this, then. At one time I think you cared for me. Do you love me now at all?'

Of course she didn't love him. In fact, she knew now that she never really had, at least not the way she'd loved Blake. But Blake Fowler was a hard act to follow. No man had ever made the impact on her or aroused her the way he had, but he'd walked out of her life, and she was certain it was for good. She hadn't tried to call him again, nor had she heard one word from him in over a month.

The truth was, Blake Fowler was simply not available to her, and now, against all her expectations, Jim was. Was she being an utter fool to turn down second best, to be left with nothing?

She gazed at him now in the glow of the light beside the front door of the house and tried to summon up some of the old affection she used to feel for him. He was a handsome man who kept himself physically fit. He was a powerful force in the political world, highly successful, dynamic personally. But she didn't love him. And in her book that meant there was no question.

The problem was how to tell him. In spite of his brilliant successes, underneath he was a very vulnerable man, thin-skinned, with only a thin veneer of ego to protect him.

The silence was becoming oppressive as he waited patiently for her to speak. Shelley knew she had to say something, but she didn't want to hurt him. When she gave him a quick covert glance, she saw that the handsome, smiling face was now creased in a frown of annoyance. Although he recovered himself quickly, it was clear he'd expected an enthusiastic acceptance.

However, he wasn't a successful politician for nothing, and his expression now became one of benevolent understanding. He even managed a low chuckle.

'I can see I've spoken too soon. I just wanted to let you know how I felt, but for now it's probably best to leave it at that. Don't give me your final answer now, and I'll give you a little room to breathe, to think things over, and wait for you to let me know your decision.'

For the next few days, Shelley couldn't get Jim's proposal off her mind. Although she certainly didn't love him and had no intention of marrying him, she still had to tell him so. From the way he'd left things, almost forbidding her to speak, she knew he'd manipulated her into that position, put the ball firmly in her court, the last place she wanted it. Why hadn't she simply rejected him that last night?

Finally she decided she'd have to risk talking it over with her mother and opening the floodgates of joy she would undoubtedly feel at the prospect of her daughter married to the governor. It was a lazy Sunday afternoon. John Dalton was upstairs having his afternoon rest, and the two women were sitting in front of the fire in the living-room idly leafing through the bulky Seattle Sunday newspaper.

'Mother,' Shelley said at last, 'I need to ask your advice about something.'

Ruth lowered the paper and gazed at her over her spectacles. 'Yes, dear? What is it?'

'Jim Carruthers has asked me to marry him,' Shelley blurted out in a rush.

'Hmm,' was the response, 'I thought he might.'

Shelley's eyes flew open. 'You did?' She laughed. 'Well, you must be psychic. I had no idea that was on his mind. Anyway, I don't quite know what to do about it.'

'Yes, I can see how it might be a problem.' Ruth lowered the newspaper and gazed at her daughter over the edge. 'Do you want to marry him?'

'No!' Shelley stated firmly. 'I have no intention of marrying him. I don't love him. But I don't know how to tell him, and I was hoping you might have some ideas.' This wasn't going at all as she'd expected. Where was the joy at having the governor for a son-in-law?

'Well, darling, if you don't love him, and don't want to marry him, I can't see that you really have a problem. Just tell him so.' Ruth paused for a moment. 'You still love Blake, don't you?'

'No!' Shelley cried. 'Of course not! Besides, even if I did, there's no hope for any kind of a future with him.' She jumped up from her chair and began pacing the room, wringing her hands. 'You're not being very helpful,' she accused, coming to stand before her mother and glaring down at her.

'I'm sorry, I wish I could help you. Perhaps...'

Just then there came a sudden series of strange sounds from upstairs—a strangled cry, followed by a heavy thud, then dead silence. Ruth Dalton leapt from her chair and clutched at her heart, her eyes stricken.

'John!' she whispered, and ran immediately towards the stairs, with Shelley following close behind her.

It turned out to be another heart attack, this one more serious than the first, but still not the killer Shelley had feared. She and her mother spent the rest of the afternoon and evening in the hospital. Once they were assured that John was out of danger, Ruth insisted on staying with him that night.

She was equally insistent that Shelley go home. The full burden of getting out the paper was with her now, and although she could see the wisdom in the decision it was with a heavy heart that she stepped inside the cold, empty house later that night.

She needed desperately to talk to someone, to feel the warmth of human support. In the past she'd always had her parents to rely on for that, but now she'd had her first taste of what it would be like when they were both gone, and a cold fear clutched at her heart. Who was there to turn to now?

The next few days were harried as she assumed full responsibility for getting out the paper. Luckily it was only a weekly, published each Friday, but there was still a lot of preparation to be done before it could be set in type, and it all fell on her shoulders.

By Thursday afternoon, she was certain it would never get to the printers on time. She wasn't even halfway through with the layout. It would be the first time in history that the paper wouldn't be delivered on schedule, and the worst of it was letting her father down.

She missed him terribly. It was one thing to try her wings under his steadying hand, and the years of solid experience behind him, even exhilarating, but quite another to be thrown back entirely on her own resources this way. She simply wasn't up to it.

She was just about ready to give up and admit defeat when she heard the front door open. 'That's all I need,' she muttered to herself. 'Another newsy item about somebody's sick cow that just has to get into this week's edition.'

She stalked out into the front office, all ready to do battle with some insistent farmer, but when she reached the door she stopped short. There, standing on the other side of the counter, was Blake Fowler, the last person she had ever expected to see again.

She put her hand to her throat. 'Blake!' she said. 'What in the world are you doing here?'

'I heard about your father,' he replied with a casual wave of one hand, 'and thought maybe you could use some help.'

She shook her head, bewildered. 'Help? How can you help?'

He laughed. 'I'm an old newspaperman, remember? I still haven't forgotten my years as copy boy and cub reporter.' He shrugged out of his jacket and swung around the counter to her side. 'Come on, let's get cracking.'

For the next four hours they worked side by side without a let-up, and by six o'clock, when the messenger arrived from the printers, the layout was all ready for delivery.

When he was gone, Shelley sank exhausted into a chair and heaved a deep sigh. 'I can't believe we really did it,' she said wearily. 'It's a miracle.'

'Well, now,' Blake said, 'it wasn't so bad, was it?' He was standing across the room from her and drinking what must have been his hundredth cup of coffee, beaming with satisfaction. 'A good day's work, I'd say.'

Now that the panic was over, she was struck once again by the oddity of his sudden appearance. She couldn't quite take in the utter incongruity of the whole situation. She'd just spent four hours at hard labour with a man she'd never expected to see again.

She watched him now as he drained the dregs of his coffee, then stretched widely, flexing the muscles of his back and shoulders. He was in his shirt-sleeves and had long since taken off his tie, leaving the top button undone. His hair was mussed, and one dark lock fell over his forehead.

'Blake,' she began slowly, 'I'm more grateful than I can ever say for your help. I couldn't have done it without you. But I can't help wondering why. I mean, I was bowled over when you simply showed up like that, out of the blue.'

For a moment he didn't say anything. Then he gave an offhand shrug. 'I already told you why I came. I heard about your father, and figured you'd need some help. How is he, by the way?'

'He's fine.' She smiled. 'Getting stronger every day, in fact, and clamouring to come home.'

'That's good. But I imagine he'll still have to take it easy for a while, perhaps for good. Do you think you can handle all this on your own?'

So that was it! 'Well, I can try,' she replied stiffly. 'If it's your investment you're worried about...'

'Shelley!' he barked, cutting her off. 'Stop it!'

He set his cup down carefully and came over to stand before her, scowling darkly down at her. 'Damn it,' he growled, 'I don't care about the investment. Do you think it matters to me whether you miss one edition? I came here to see you.'

She gazed up at him blankly. 'I don't understand.'

He perched on the edge of her desk. 'No? Well, let's see if I can clarify it. I found I couldn't live without you. Is that plain enough?'

Her heart gave a great lurch. But why was he so angry? It was as though each word had been dragged out of him painfully. She eyed him warily, fighting down the hope that rose within her. She had to keep her wits about her or she'd end up worse off than she was before.

'That all depends,' she said carefully. She shrugged. 'I mean, some weeks ago you simply walked out of my life. In the meantime I haven't heard one word from you. You can't just walk back in and expect to take up where you left off. Besides, a lot has happened since then.'

He quirked a heavy dark eyebrow at her. 'Such as?'

'Well, for one thing, Jim Carruthers has asked me to marry him.'

Blake reared his head back sharply as though he'd been struck. 'I see,' he said at last in a flat voice.

He turned away from her then and went over to pour himself another cup of coffee. He stood with his back to her, his cup raised in one hand, the other resting on his hip. When he'd finished the coffee, he set the cup down and turned to face her again, his face a blank.

'And are you going to?' he asked distantly.

'I don't know. I haven't decided.' That wasn't quite true, of course. She'd known from the moment he'd asked her that she had no intention of marrying Jim, but she hadn't really told him so yet.

He came back to her then, striding rapidly across the room, his face like thunder, the brilliant blue eyes flashing fire. 'God, Shelley,' he rasped angrily, 'I thought you'd learned by now. How can you even think of trusting a man who treated you the way Jim Carruthers did? Are you some kind of glutton for punishment?'

She glared up at him. 'Oh, and I suppose you think I should have trusted you. Is that it?'

'I never lied to you. Or broke any promises.'

'No,' she drawled sarcastically. 'Of course not. All you ever wanted was to get me in bed.'

'Well, I didn't succeed, did I?' he rejoined hotly. 'And yet I still hung around—God knows why. And I've come back.' Then his face softened, and he leaned down to gaze into her eyes. 'I still care about you, Shelley, and I don't want to lose you.'

The gentleness in his voice set her heart fluttering wildly. Gazing up at him now, she thought she loved him more at that moment than ever before. But she also knew it was hopeless. His mind was simply closed to commitment. He was incapable of settling for just one woman in his life, and her pride wouldn't let her enter into an affair with him or share him or force him into promises he didn't want to make.

She would have to let him go. There was no other way, and as the tears welled up behind her eyes she turned her head.

'I'm sorry,' she said stiffly, 'I can't play your games, Blake. They're way out of my league.'

He clamped his hands on her shoulders and forced her around to face him. 'Haven't you heard one word I've been saying?' he ground out through his teeth.

She turned on him. 'Apparently not,' she retorted. 'But of course that's my fault, isn't it? You've made yourself perfectly clear—as mud, that is!'

'All right!' he exclaimed. 'How about this? I want you to marry me. Is that clear enough?'

Her mouth fell open and her head began to whirl, overcome by a piercing emotion she couldn't quite identify. Did he mean it? Or was his male ego so wounded at the thought of losing her to Jim that he was using one last desperate ploy to get his own way?

She looked down at her hands, twisting in her lap. 'Well,' she muttered, 'I'm not so sure I want to marry you.'

He groaned loudly. 'Then will you please just tell me what you do want?' he demanded heatedly.

She jumped to her feet, put her hands on her hips and glared up at him. 'Well, it would be nice to think you cared something about me. Or is that too much to ask?' She felt sudden hot tears smarting in her eyes and turned quickly away from him.

In a moment she heard him come up behind her, felt his hands on her shoulders. 'Now,' he said, turning her around to face him, 'listen carefully, because I mean every word.' He sucked in a lungful of air. 'Darling, I love you. Will you please marry me?'

Shelley couldn't help laughing, even through her tears. The contrast between the ardent words of love and the defiant tone of voice were so incongruous that it was too funny for words. When the first giggle escaped her lips, she put a hand over her mouth to stifle it, but it was obviously too late.

Blake's brow creased ominously, his jaw hardened and his eyes narrowed into slits. He stood there glaring down at her, looking far more like a man who could cheerfully have strangled her with his bare hands than he did an ardent lover. Then, imperceptibly, the corners of his own mouth began to twitch, and in a moment they were both laughing openly.

Finally, when they'd settled down, he crossed his arms in front of him and gazed down at her, still smiling. 'So,' he said, 'are you going to marry me or what?'

Dead serious now, she looked up at him, her eyes searching his. 'Are you sure, Blake?' she murmured.

He reached out to put his hands on her shoulders. 'I've never been more sure of anything in my life. Don't you believe me? My God, woman, after what I've just put myself through? I've never even proposed to anyone before in my life.'

'Oh, Blake!' she cried happily. 'Of course I'll marry you.' Then her face clouded. 'But what am I going to do about Jim?'

He waved a hand in the air, dismissing Jim. 'Oh, that's easy. Just write and tell him you're not in love with him and have decided not to marry him. His ego can stand to be taken down a peg or two. It might even do him good.'

'Not to mention the boost it'll give your own ego to get one up on him,' she commented drily.

'Ah,' he said in an admiring voice, 'you know me so well. You'd think we'd been married for years. Now come here and let me kiss you.'

'There's something else we need to talk about first,' she said, evading his grasp. 'I can't leave the paper now, with my father sick. In fact, I don't really want to. I love the work.'

'You don't have to,' he replied promptly. 'The company decided to buy the ski lodge, and I'll be spending most of my time up here anyway. We'll hire you some competent help, and can shuttle back and forth between here and the city.' He waved a hand in the air, dismissing the whole subject. 'It's a minor matter, easily worked out. The only real question is whether you love me.'

'How can you ask?' she said, stunned. 'Of course I do.'

'Well, it wouldn't hurt you to tell me so, would it?'

She threw her arms around him, laughing up into his face. 'I love you madly, passionately, hopelessly,' she cried. 'I always have, and I always will. There, is that good enough?'

'It'll do,' he murmured. He lowered himself down into her chair and reached out for her. 'Now come here and let me kiss you properly.'

She sank down on to his lap and twined her arms around his neck as he enfolded her closely. At the first touch of his lips on hers, a touch she had never expected to feel again, she went limp inside. This was where she belonged, but a busy newspaper office was not the most ideal place for a romantic interlude, and when his hand began to snake up underneath her blouse she sat bolt upright.

'Tell me something, Blake,' she said.

'Hmm?' he murmured, his eyes half closed, not really paying attention, his hands fumbling with the clasp of her bra.

'Why did you go off like that without a word? Were you so angry that I refused to stay at the ski lodge with you that night?'

He'd finally managed the clasp and his hand was making slow circles around the fullness of one breast. When he bent his head down, she knew she'd be lost in a moment if she didn't stop him now. She put her hands on his head and pulled it up.

'Blake, will you please answer my question? Or are you trying to avoid it?'

'Ouch!' he said, laughing. 'You've scored again. All right——' his expression grew suddenly serious '—to answer your question, I went off for the simple reason that I felt you needed more time, more room, to make up your mind what you really wanted, without my admittedly disturbing presence to influence you. I told you once I wouldn't play second fiddle to any man. I needed to know that in some hidden recess of your heart you weren't still hung up on Jim Carruthers. I didn't want you on the rebound.'

With a heart full of love, she nestled her head on his shoulder. She believed him, but still couldn't resist teasing him a little. 'That was very noble of you, darling, but are you absolutely positive there wasn't just a trace of panic at the "C" word? You know, commitment?'

He chuckled deep in his throat. 'Perhaps. But I came back, didn't I?'

'That you did,' she murmured happily. 'Such a brave boy it is.'

'Are you laughing at me?'

'Yes, I am,' she replied promptly. 'How does it feel?'

His hands had snaked beneath her blouse again, and begun stroking sensuously across her bare skin. 'It feels great,' he said, and lowered his head to her breast.

Two weeks later they were married quietly in the small church in town. Shelley's father was well enough by then to attend, which made it perfect. After the small reception they drove to the ski lodge, where they were to spend their honeymoon.

As she lay in bed that night waiting for Blake, Shelley felt her heart full to bursting. She'd bought a wickedly seductive nightgown for the occasion, a flesh-coloured sheer georgette with tiny straps holding up a bodice that moulded her high, firm breasts and plunged low into the deep valley between them.

When he emerged from the bathroom after his shower, dressed only in a loose terry robe, still towelling his damp hair, a feeling of shyness gripped her.

'Ah, Mrs Fowler,' he said, coming over to sit beside her on the bed and leering down at her. 'Now I've got you where I've wanted you since the first moment I laid eyes on you.' He reached down and placed a hand possessively over her breast, moving it seductively over the thin fabric.

'Blake!' she cried, covering the hand with her own. 'Is that all I am to you? A sex object?'

'Well, no,' he said, grinning wickedly. 'But I'll have to admit it's a pretty important factor.' The hand on her breast stilled, and his expression grew grave. 'Only I'd hardly use that term. You're not an object to me at all, darling, but a vibrant, intelligent, spunky woman, and I adore you.'

Slowly he lowered one strap of her gown and brushed aside the wisp of material that still covered her. His hand came back to her bare breast, moulding the soft fullness, fingering the taut peak. Then his head came down and he kissed her, a tender kiss that pierced her heart with love.

As the kiss became more urgent, his hands began to move feverishly over her body, until finally the nightgown was cast aside. For a few long seconds he gazed down at her bare body, the bright blue eyes glittering with passion. Then, slowly, he shrugged out of his robe and stood naked before her.

Shelley gazed at him with adoration in her eyes. She'd never seen such a beautiful sight, the broad shoulders, strongly muscled chest and flat stomach, every inch of the tall form proud and hard in its intensely masculine arousal. With a little cry she held out her arms to him. He lowered himself carefully over her, leaning on his elbows, gazing down into her eyes.

'I love you, darling,' he breathed.

'And I love you.'

Then began the slow dance of love, the taking and the giving, the thrusting and the release, until they were joined together, fully man and wife.

# HARLEQUIN ROMANCE®

*brings you*

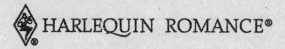

*More Romances Celebrating Love, Families and Children!*

Following on from Rosemary Gibson's *No Ties*,
Harlequin Romance #3344, this month we're bringing
you *A Valentine for Daisy*, Harlequin Romance #3347,
which we know you will enjoy reading! It's a wonderful
Betty Neels story, all about two adorable twins Josh and
Katie who play their part in Daisy finding true love
at last!

**Watch out for these titles:**

| March | #3351 | *Leonie's Luck* | Emma Goldrick |
| April | #3357 | *The Baby Business* | Rebecca Winters |
| May | #3359 | *Bachelor's Family* | Jessica Steele |

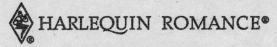
# HARLEQUIN ROMANCE®

Starting in March, we are bringing you a brand-new series—Sealed with a Kiss. We've all written SWAK at some time on a love letter, and in these books the love story always concerns a letter—one way or another!

We've chosen RITA nominee Leigh Michaels's *Invitation to Love* (Harlequin Romance #3352) as the first title and will be bringing you one every month, right through to Christmas!

Watch for *Invitation to Love* by Leigh Michaels in March. And don't miss any of these exciting Sealed with a Kiss titles, by your favorite Harlequin Romance authors:

| | | | |
|---|---|---|---|
| April | #3355 | Dearest Love | Betty Neels |
| May | #3360 | P.S. I Love You | Valerie Parv |
| June | #3366 | Mail-Order Bridegroom | Day Leclaire |
| July | #3370 | Wanted: Wife and Mother | Barbara McMahon |

Available wherever Harlequin books are sold.

# HARLEQUIN®

Don't miss these Harlequin favorites by some of our most distinguished authors!
And now, you can receive a discount by ordering two or more titles!

| | | | |
|---|---|---|---|
| HT#25577 | WILD LIKE THE WIND by Janice Kaiser | $2.99 | ☐ |
| HT#25589 | THE RETURN OF CAINE O'HALLORAN by JoAnn Ross | $2.99 | ☐ |
| HP#11626 | THE SEDUCTION STAKES by Lindsay Armstrong | $2.99 | ☐ |
| HP#11647 | GIVE A MAN A BAD NAME by Roberta Leigh | $2.99 | ☐ |
| HR#03293 | THE MAN WHO CAME FOR CHRISTMAS by Bethany Campbell | $2.89 | ☐ |
| HR#03308 | RELATIVE VALUES by Jessica Steele | $2.89 | ☐ |
| SR#70589 | CANDY KISSES by Muriel Jensen | $3.50 | ☐ |
| SR#70598 | WEDDING INVITATION by Marisa Carroll | $3.50 U.S. $3.99 CAN. | ☐ |
| HI#22230 | CACHE POOR by Margaret St. George | $3.50 | ☐ |
| HAR#16515 | NO ROOM AT THE INN by Linda Randall Wisdom | $3.50 | ☐ |
| HAR#16520 | THE ADVENTURESS by M.J. Rodgers | $3.50 | ☐ |
| HS#28795 | PIECES OF SKY by Marianne Willman | $3.99 | ☐ |
| HS#28824 | A WARRIOR'S WAY by Margaret Moore | $3.99 U.S. $4.50 CAN. | ☐ |

(limited quantities available on certain titles)

| | AMOUNT | $ |
|---|---|---|
| DEDUCT: | 10% DISCOUNT FOR 2+ BOOKS | $ |
| ADD: | POSTAGE & HANDLING | $ |
| | ($1.00 for one book, 50¢ for each additional) | |
| | APPLICABLE TAXES* | $_____ |
| | TOTAL PAYABLE | $_____ |
| | (check or money order—please do not send cash) | |

To order, complete this form and send it, along with a check or money order for the total above, payable to Harlequin Books, to: **In the U.S.:** 3010 Walden Avenue, P.O. Box 9047, Buffalo, NY 14269-9047; **In Canada:** P.O. Box 613, Fort Erie, Ontario, L2A 5X3.

Name:_____

Address: _____ City:_____

State/Prov.:_____ Zip/Postal Code:_____

*New York residents remit applicable sales taxes.
 Canadian residents remit applicable GST and provincial taxes.

HBACK-JM2

Fifty red-blooded, white-hot, true-blue hunks
from every State in the Union!

Look for MEN MADE IN AMERICA! Written by some
of our most popular authors, these stories feature some
of the strongest, sexiest men, each from a different state
in the union!

Two titles available every month at your favorite
retail outlet.

In January, look for:

WITHIN REACH by Marilyn Pappano (New Mexico)
IN GOOD FAITH by Judith McWilliams (New York)

In February, look for:

THE SECURITY MAN by Dixie Browning
(North Carolina)
A CLASS ACT by Kathleen Eagle
(North Dakota)

## You won't be able to resist MEN MADE IN AMERICA!

**Where do you find hot Texas nights, smooth Texas charm and dangerously sexy cowboys?**

Crystal Creek reverberates with the exciting rhythm of Texas. Each story features the rugged individuals who live and love in the Lone Star state.

"...Crystal Creek wonderfully evokes the hot days and steamy nights of a small Texas community...impossible to put down until the last page is turned."
—*Romantic Times*

**Praise for Bethany Campbell's** *Rhinestone Cowboy*

"...this is a poignant, heart-warming story of love and redemption. One that Crystal Creek followers will wish to grab and hold on to."
—*Affaire de Coeur*

"Bethany Campbell is surely one of the brightest stars of this series."
—*Affaire de Coeur*

Don't miss the final book in this exciting series. Look for
**LONESTAR STATE OF MIND** by BETHANY CAMPBELL

Available in February wherever Harlequin books are sold.

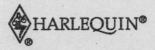